The FAMOUS FIVE *are*
Julian, Dick, George (Georgina by rights),
Anne, and Timothy the dog

If Uncle Quentin had had the
top-heavy ash tree lopped, the gale
would not have brought it crashing
down on to Kirrin Cottage, and then
the Five would not have gone to
Smuggler's Top to stay with
Sooty Lenoir and his eccentric father.

But once there, queer and highly
suspicious things seemed to happen,
one after the other. Timmy, too,
had his fair share of excitement,
in and out of underground passages,
and on the surrounding sea-marshes.

Enid Blyton

Five Go To
Smuggler's Top

Illustrated by Eileen Soper

AN ALADDIN BOOK
Atheneum

Five Go to Smuggler's Top
FIRST PUBLISHED 1945
THIS EDITION COPYRIGHT © 1972 DARRELL WATERS LIMITED
ALL RIGHTS RESERVED
MANUFACTURED IN THE UNITED STATES OF AMERICA BY
THE MURRAY PRINTING COMPANY
FORGE VILLAGE, MASSACHUSETTS
ISBN 0-689-70323-6

CONTENTS

BACK TO KIRRIN COTTAGE

ONE fine day right at the beginning of the Easter holidays, four children and a dog travelled by train together.

'Soon be there now,' said Julian, a tall strong boy, with a determined face.

'Woof,' said Timothy the dog, getting excited, and trying to look out of the window too.

'Get down, Tim,' said Julian. 'Let Anne have a look.'

Anne was his young sister. She put her head out of the window. 'We're coming into Kirrin Station!' she said. 'I do hope Aunt Fanny will be there to meet us.'

'Of course she will!' said Georgina, her cousin. She looked more like a boy than a girl, for she wore her hair very short, and it curled close about her head. She too had a determined face, like Julian. She pushed Anne away and looked out of the window.

'It's nice to be going home,' she said. 'I love school – but it will be fun to be at Kirrin Cottage and perhaps sail out to Kirrin Island and visit the castle there. We haven't been since last summer.'

'Dick's turn to look out now,' said Julian, turning to his younger brother, a boy with a pleasant face, sitting reading in a corner. 'We're just coming into sight of Kirrin, Dick. Can't you stop reading for a second?'

'It's such an exciting book,' said Dick, and shut it with a clap. 'The most exciting adventure story I've ever read!'

'Pooh! I bet it's not as exciting as some of the adventures *we've* had!' said Anne, at once.

It was quite true that the five of them, counting in

7

Timmy the dog, who always shared everything with them, had had the most amazing adventures together. But now it looked as if they were going to have nice quiet holidays, going for long walks over the cliffs, and perhaps sailing out in George's boat to their island of Kirrin.

'I've worked jolly hard at school this term,' said Julian. 'I could do with a holiday!'

'You've gone thin,' said Georgina. Nobody called her that. They all called her George. She would never answer to any other name. Julian grinned.

'Well, I'll soon get fat at Kirrin Cottage, don't you worry! Aunt Fanny will see to that. She's a great one for trying to fatten people up. It will be nice to see your mother again, George. She's an awfully good sort.'

'Yes. I hope Father will be in a good temper these holls,' said George. 'He ought to be because he has just finished some new experiments, Mother says, which have been quite successful.'

George's father was a scientist, always working out new ideas. He liked to be quiet, and sometimes he flew into a temper when he could not get the peace he needed or things did not go exactly as he wanted them to. The children often thought that hot-tempered Georgina was very like her father! She too could fly into fierce tempers when things did not go right for her.

Aunt Fanny was there to meet them. The four children jumped out on the platform and rushed to hug her. George got there first. She was very fond of her gentle mother, who had so often tried to shield her when her father got angry with her. Timmy pranced round, barking in delight. He adored George's mother.

She patted him, and he tried to stand up and lick her face. 'Timmy's bigger than ever!' she said, laughing. 'Down, old boy! You'll knock me over.'

Timmy was certainly a big dog. All the children loved him, for he was loyal, loving and faithful. His brown eyes looked from one to the other, enjoying the children's excitement. Timmy shared in it, as he shared in every-thing.

But the person he loved most, of course, was his mistress, George. She had had him since he was a small puppy. She took him to school with her each term, for she and Anne went to a boarding-school that allowed pets. Otherwise George would most certainly have refused to go!

They set off to Kirrin in the pony-trap. It was very windy and cold, and the children shivered and pulled their coats tightly round them.

'It's awfully cold,' said Anne, her teeth beginning to chatter. 'Colder than in the winter!'

'It's the wind,' said her aunt, and tucked a rug round her. 'It's been getting very strong the last day or two. The fishermen have pulled their boats high up the beach for fear of a big storm.'

The children saw the boats pulled right up as they passed the beach where they had bathed so often. They did not feel like bathing now. It made them shiver even to think of it.

The wind howled over the sea. Great scudding clouds raced overhead. The waves pounded on the beach and made a terrific noise. It excited Timmy, who began to bark.

'Be quiet, Tim,' said George, patting him. 'You will have to learn to be a good quiet dog now we are home again, or Father will be cross with you. Is Father very busy, Mother?'

'Very,' said her mother. 'But he's going to do very

little work now you are coming home. He thought he
would like to go for walks with you, or go out in the boat,
if the weather calms down.'

The children looked at one another. Uncle Quentin
was not the best of companions. He had no sense of
humour, and when the children went off into fits of
laughter, as they did twenty times a day or more, he could
not see the joke at all.

'It looks as if these holls won't be quite so jolly if Uncle
Quentin parks himself on us most of the time,' said Dick
in a low voice to Julian.

'Sh,' said Julian, afraid that his aunt would hear, and
be hurt. George frowned.

'Oh Mother! Father will be bored stiff if he comes
with us – and we'll be bored too.'

George was very outspoken, and could never learn to
keep a guard on her tongue. Her mother sighed. 'Don't
talk like that, dear. I daresay your father will get tired
of going with you after a bit. But it does him good to have
a bit of young life about him.'

'Here we are!' said Julian, as the trap stopped outside
an old house. 'Kirrin Cottage! My word, how the wind
is howling round it, Aunt Fanny!'

'Yes. It made a terrible noise last night,' said his aunt.
'You take the trap round to the back, Julian, when we've
got the things out. Oh, here's your uncle to help!'

Uncle Quentin came out, a tall, clever-looking man,
with rather frowning eyebrows. He smiled at the children
and kissed George and Anne.

'Welcome to Kirrin Cottage!' he said. 'I'm quite glad
your mother and father are away, Anne, because now
we shall have you all here once again!'

Soon they were sitting round the table eating a big tea.
Aunt Fanny always got ready a fine meal for their first

one, for she knew they were very hungry after their long
journey in the train.

Even George was satisfied at last, and leaned back in
her chair, wishing she could manage just one more of
her mother's delicious new-made buns.

Timmy sat close to her. He was not supposed to be fed
at meal-times but it was really surprising how many tit-
bits found their way to him under the table!

The wind howled round the house. The windows
rattled, the doors shook, and the mats lifted themselves
up and down as the draught got under them.

'They look as if they've got snakes wriggling under-
neath them,' said Anne. Timmy watched them and
growled. He was a clever dog, but he did not know why
the mats wriggled in such a queer way.

'I hope the wind will die down tonight,' said Aunt
Fanny. 'It kept me awake last night. Julian dear, you
look rather thin. Have you been working hard? I must
fatten you up.'

The children laughed. 'Just what we thought you'd
say, Mother!' said George. 'Goodness, what's that?'

They all sat still, startled. There was a loud bumping
noise on the roof, and Timmy put up his ears and growled
fiercely.

'A tile off the roof,' said Uncle Quentin. 'How tiresome! We shall have to get the loose tiles seen to, Fanny,
when the storm is over, or the rain will come in.'

The children rather hoped that their uncle would retire
to his study after tea, as he usually did, but this time
he didn't. They wanted to play a game, but it wasn't
much good with Uncle Quentin there. He really wasn't
any good at all, not even at such a simple game as
snap.

'Do you know a boy called Pierre Lenoir?' suddenly

asked Uncle Quentin, taking a letter from his pocket. 'I believe he goes to your school and Dick's, Julian.'

'Pierre Lenoir – oh you mean old Sooty,' said Julian. 'Yes – he's in Dick's form, sir. Mad as a hatter.'

'Sooty! Now why do you call him that?' said Uncle Quentin. 'It seems a silly name for a boy.'

'If you saw him you wouldn't think so,' said Dick, with a laugh. 'He's awfully dark! Hair as black as soot, eyes like bits of coal, eyebrows that look as if they've been put in with charcoal. And his name means "The black one," doesn't it? Le-Noir – that's French for black.'

'Yes. Quite true. But what a name to give anyone – *Sooty!*' said Uncle Quentin. 'Well, I've been having quite a lot of correspondence with this boy's father. He and I are interested in the same scientific matters. In fact, I've asked him whether he wouldn't like to come and stay with me a few days – and bring his boy, Pierre.'

'Oh really!' said Dick, looking quite pleased. 'Well, it wouldn't be bad sport to have old Sooty here, Uncle. But he's quite mad. He never does as he's told, he climbs like a monkey, and he can be awfully cheeky. I don't know if you'd like him much.'

Uncle Quentin looked sorry he had asked Sooty after he had heard what Dick had to say. He didn't like cheeky boys. Nor did he like mad ones.

'H'm,' he said, putting the letter away. 'I wish I'd asked you about the boy first, before suggesting to his father that he might bring him with him. But perhaps I can prevent him coming.'

'No, don't, Father,' said George, who rather liked the sound of Sooty Lenoir. 'Let's have him. He could come out with us and liven things up!'

'We'll see,' said her father, who had already made up his mind on no account to have the boy at Kirrin Cottage, if he was mad, climbed everywhere, and was cheeky. George was enough of a handful without a madcap of a boy egging her on!

Much to the children's relief Uncle Quentin retired to read by himself about eight o'clock. Aunt Fanny looked at the clock.

'Time for Anne to go to bed,' she said. 'And you too, George.'

'Just one good game of Slap-Down Patience, all of us playing it together, Mother!' said George. 'Come on — you play it too. It's our first evening at home. Anyway, I shan't sleep for ages, with this gale howling round! Come on, Mother — one good game, then we'll go to bed. Julian's been yawning like anything already!'

A SHOCK IN THE NIGHT

It was nice to climb up the steep stairs to their familiar bedrooms that night. All the children were yawning widely. Their long train journey had tired them.

'If only this awful wind would stop!' said Anne, pulling the curtain aside and looking out into the night. 'There's a little moon, George. It keeps bobbing out between the scurrying clouds.'

'Let it bob!' said George, scrambling into bed. 'I'm jolly cold. Hurry, Anne, or you'll catch a chill at that window.'

'Don't the waves make a noise?' said Anne, still at the window. 'And the gale in the old ash-tree is making a whistling, howling sound, and bending it right over.'

'Timmy, hurry up and get on my bed,' commanded George, screwing up her cold toes. 'That's one good thing about being at home, Anne. I can have Timmy on my bed! He's far better than a hot water bottle.'

'You're not supposed to have him on your bed at home, any more than you're supposed to at school,' said Anne, curling up in bed. 'Aunt Fanny thinks he sleeps in his basket over there.'

'Well, I can't stop him coming on my bed at night, can I, if he doesn't want to sleep in his basket?' said George. 'That's right, Timmy darling. Make my feet warm. Where's your nose? Let me pat it. Good-night, Tim. Good-night, Anne.'

'Good-night,' said Anne, sleepily. 'I hope that Sooty boy comes, don't you? He does sound fun.'

'Yes. And anyway Father would stay in with Mr. Lenoir, the boy's father, and not come out with us,' said George. 'Father doesn't mean to, but he does spoil things somehow.'

'He's not very good at laughing,' said Anne. 'He's too serious.'

A loud bang made both girls jump. 'That's the bathroom door!' said George, with a groan. 'One of the boys must have left it open. That's the sort of noise that drives Father mad! There it goes again!'

'Well, let Julian or Dick shut it,' said Anne, who was now beginning to feel nice and warm. But Julian and Dick were thinking that George or Anne might shut it, so nobody got out of bed to see to the banging door.

Very soon Uncle Quentin's voice roared up the stairs, louder than the gale.

'Shut that door, one of you! How can I work with that noise going on!'

All four children jumped out of bed like a shot. Timmy leapt off George's bed. Everyone fell over him as they rushed to the bathroom door. There was a lot of giggling and scuffling. Then Uncle Quentin's footsteps were heard on the stairs and the five fled silently to their rooms.

The gale still roared. Uncle Quentin and Aunt Fanny came up to bed. The bedroom door flew out of Uncle Quentin's hand and slammed itself shut so violently that a vase leapt off a nearby shelf.

Uncle Quentin leapt too, startled. 'This wretched gale!' he said, fiercely. 'Never known one like it all the time we've been here. If it gets much worse the fishermen's boats will be smashed up, even though they've pulled them as high up the beach as possible.'

'It will blow itself out soon, dear,' said Aunt Fanny,

soothingly. 'Probably by the time morning comes it will be quite calm.'

But she was wrong. The gale did not blow itself out that night. Instead it raged round the house even more fiercely, shrieking and howling like a live thing. Nobody could sleep. Timmy kept up a continuous low growling, for he did not like the shakes and rattles and howls.

Towards dawn the wind seemed in a fury. Anne thought it sounded as if it was in a horrible temper, out to do all the harm it could. She lay and trembled, half-frightened.

Suddenly there was a strange noise. It was a loud and woeful groaning and creaking, like someone in great pain. The two girls sat up, terrified. What could it be?

The boys heard it too. Julian leapt out of bed and ran to the window. Outside stood the old ash tree, tall and black in the fitful moonlight. It was gradually bending over!

'It's the ash! It's falling!' yelled Julian, almost startling Dick out of his wits. 'It's falling, I tell you. It'll crash on the house! Quick, warn the girls!'

Shouting at the top of his voice, Julian raced out of his door on to the landing. 'Uncle! Aunt! George and Anne! Come downstairs quickly! The ash tree is falling!'

George jumped out of bed, snatched at her dressing-gown, and raced to the door, yelling to Anne. The little girl was soon with her. Timmy ran in front. At the door of Aunt Fanny's bedroom Uncle Quentin appeared, tall and amazed, wrapping his dressing-gown round him.

'What's all this noise? Julian, what's – ?'

'Aunt Fanny! Come downstairs – the ash tree is falling! Listen to its terrible groans and creaks!' yelled Julian, almost beside himself with impatience. 'It'll smash

in the room and the bedrooms! Listen, here it comes!'

Everyone fled downstairs as, with an appalling wail, the great ash tree hauled up its roots and fell heavily on to Kirrin Cottage. There was a terrible crash, and the sound of tiles slipping to the ground everywhere.

'Oh dear!' said poor Aunt Fanny, covering her eyes. 'I knew something would happen! Quentin, we ought to have had that ash tree topped. I knew it would fall in a great gale like this. What has it done to the roof?'

After the great crash there had come other smaller noises, sounds of things falling, thuds and little smashing noises. The children could not imagine what was happening. Timmy was thoroughly angry, and barked loudly. Uncle Quentin slapped his hand angrily on the table, and made everyone jump.

'Stop that dog barking! I'll turn him out!' But nothing would stop Timmy barking or growling that night, and George at last pushed him into the warm kitchen, and shut the door on him.

'I feel like barking or growling myself,' said Anne, who knew exactly what Timmy felt like. 'Julian, has the tree broken in the roof?'

Uncle Quentin took a powerful torch and went carefully up the stairs to the landing to see what damage had been done. He came down looking rather pale.

'The tree has crashed through the attic, smashed the roof in, and wrecked the girls' bedroom,' he said. 'A big branch has penetrated the boys' room too, but not badly. But the girls' room is ruined! They would have been killed if they had been in their beds.'

Everyone was silent. It was an awful thought that George and Anne had had such a narrow escape.

'Good thing I yelled my head off to warn them, then,' said Julian, cheerfully, seeing how white Anne had gone.

'Cheer up, Anne – think what a tale you'll have to tell at school next term.'

'I think some hot cocoa would do us all good,' said Aunt Fanny, pulling herself together, though she felt very shaken. 'I'll go and make some. Quentin, see if the fire is still alight in your study. We want a little warmth!'

The fire was still alight. Everyone crowded round it. They welcomed Aunt Fanny when she came in with some steaming milk-cocoa.

Anne looked curiously round the room as she sat sipping her drink. This was where her uncle did his work, his very clever work. He wrote his difficult books here, books which Anne could not understand at all. He drew his queer diagrams here, and made many strange experiments.

But just at the moment Uncle Quentin did not look very clever. He looked rather ashamed, somehow. Anne soon knew why.

'Quentin, it is a mercy none of us was hurt or killed,' said Aunt Fanny, looking at him rather sternly. 'I told you a dozen times you should get that ash tree topped. I knew it was too big and heavy to withstand a great gale. I was always afraid it would blow down on the house.'

'Yes, I know, my dear,' said Uncle Quentin, stirring his cup of cocoa very vigorously. 'But I was so busy these last months.'

'You always make that an excuse for not doing urgent things,' said Aunt Fanny, with a sigh. 'I shall have to manage things myself in the future. I can't risk our lives like this!'

'Well, a thing like this would only happen once in a blue moon!' cried Uncle Quentin, getting angry. Then he calmed down, seeing that Aunt Fanny was really shocked and upset, very near to tears. He put down his cocoa and slipped his arm round her.

'You've had a terrible shock,' he said. 'Don't you worry about things. Maybe they won't be so bad when morning comes.'

'Oh, Quentin – they'll be much worse!' said his wife. 'Where shall we sleep tonight, all of us, and what shall we do till the roof and upstairs rooms are repaired? The children have only just come home. The house will be full of workmen for weeks! I don't know how I'm going to manage.'

'Leave it all to me!' said Uncle Quentin. 'I'll settle everything. Don't you worry. I'm sorry about this, very sorry, particularly as it's my fault. But I'll straighten things out for everyone, you just see!'

Aunt Fanny didn't really believe him, but she was grateful for his comforting. The children listened in silence, drinking their hot cocoa. Uncle Quentin was so very clever, and knew so many things – but it was so like him to neglect something urgent like cutting off the top of the old ash tree. Sometimes he didn't seem to live in this world at all!

It was no use going up to bed! The rooms upstairs were either completely ruined, or so messed up with bits and pieces, and clouds of dust, that it was impossible to sleep there. Aunt Fanny began to pile rugs on sofas. There was one in the study, a big one in the sitting-room and a smaller one in the dining-room. She found a camp bed in a cupboard and, with Julian's help, put that up too.

'We'll just have to do the best we can,' she said. 'There isn't much left of the night, but we'll get a little sleep if we can! The gale is not nearly so wild now.'

'No – it's done all the damage it can, so it's satisfied,'

said Uncle Quentin, grimly. 'Well, we'll talk things over in the morning.'

The children found it very difficult to go to sleep after such an excitement, tired though they were. Anne felt worried. How could they all stay at Kirrin Cottage now? It wouldn't be fair on Aunt Fanny. But they couldn't go home because her father and mother were both away and the house was shut up for a month.

'I hope we shan't be sent back to school,' thought Anne, trying to get comfortable on the sofa. 'It would be too awful, after having left there, and started off so gaily for the holidays.'

George was afraid of that, too. She felt sure that they would all be packed back to their schools the next morning. That would mean that she and Anne wouldn't see Julian and Dick any more those holidays, for the boys, of course, went to a different school.

Timmy was the only one who didn't worry about things. He lay on George's feet, snoring a little, quite happy. So long as he was with George he didn't really mind *where* he went!

UNCLE QUENTIN HAS AN IDEA

NEXT morning the wind was still high, but the fury of the gale was gone. The fishermen on the beach were relieved to find that their boats had suffered very little damage. But word soon went round about the accident to Kirrin Cottage, and a few sightseers came up to marvel at the sight of the great, uprooted tree, lying heavily on the little house.

The children rather enjoyed the importance of relating how nearly they had escaped with their lives. In the light of day it was surprising what damage the big tree had done. It had cracked the roof of the house like an egg-shell, and the rooms upstairs were in a terrible mess.

The woman who came up from the village to help Aunt Fanny during the day exclaimed at the sight: 'Why, Mam, it'll take weeks to set that right!' she said. 'Have you got on to the builders, Mam? I'd get them up here right away and let them see what's to be done.'

'*I'm* seeing to things, Mrs. Daly,' said Uncle Quentin. 'My wife has had a great shock. She is not fit to see to things herself. The first thing to do is to decide what is to happen to the children. They can't remain here while there are no usable bedrooms.'

'They had better go back to school, poor things,' said Aunt Fanny.

'No. I've a better idea than that,' said Uncle Quentin, fishing a letter out of his pocket. 'Much better. I've had a letter from that fellow Lenoir this morning – you know, the one who's interested in the same kind of experiments as I am. He says – er, wait a minute, I'll read you the bit. Yes, here it is.'

Uncle Quentin read it out: 'It is most kind of you to suggest my coming to stay with you and bringing my boy Pierre. Allow me to extend hospitality to you and your children also. I do not know how many you have, but all are welcome here in this big house. My Pierre will be glad of company, and so will his sister, Marybelle.'

Uncle Quentin looked up triumphantly at his wife. 'There you are! I call that a most generous invitation! It couldn't have come at a better time. We'll pack the whole of the children off to this fellow's house.'

'But Quentin – you can't possibly do that! Why, we don't know anything about him or his family!' said Aunt Fanny.

'His boy goes to the same school as Julian and Dick, and I know Lenoir is a remarkable, clever fellow,' said Uncle Quentin, as if that was all that really mattered. 'I'll telephone him now. What's his number?'

Aunt Fanny felt helpless in face of her husband's sudden determination to settle everything himself. He was ashamed because it was his forgetfulness that had brought on the accident to the house. Now he was going to show that he *could* see to things if he liked. She heard him telephoning, and frowned. How could they possibly send off the children to a strange place like that?

Uncle Quentin put down the receiver, and went to find his wife, looking jubilant and very pleased with himself.

'It's all settled,' he said. 'Lenoir is delighted, most delighted. Says he loves children about the place, and so does his wife, and his two will be thrilled to have them. If we can hire a car today, they can go at once.'

'But, Quentin – we *can't* let them go off like that to strange people! They'll hate it! I shouldn't be surprised if George refuses to go,' said his wife.

'Oh – that reminds me. She's not to take Timothy,' said Uncle Quentin. 'Apparently Lenoir doesn't like dogs.'

'Well, then, you know George won't go!' said his wife. 'That's foolish, Quentin. George won't go anywhere without Timmy.'

'She'll have to, this time,' said Uncle Quentin, quite determined that George should not upset all his marvellous plans. 'Here are the children. I'll ask them what *they* feel about going, and see what they say!'

He called them into his study. They came in, feeling sure that they were to hear bad news – probably they were all to return to school!

'You remember that boy I spoke to you about last

night?' began Uncle Quentin. 'Pierre Lenoir. You had some absurd name for him.'

'Sooty,' said Dick and Julian together.

'Ah yes, Sooty. Well, his father has kindly invited you all to go and stay with him at Smuggler's Top,' said Uncle Quentin.

The children were astonished.

'*Smuggler's Top!*' said Dick, his fancy caught by the queer name. 'What's Smuggler's Top?'

'The name of his house,' said Uncle Quentin. 'It's very old, built on the top of a queer hill surrounded by marshes over which the sea once flowed. The hill was once an island, but now it's just a tall hill rising up from the marsh. Smuggling went on there in the old days. It's a very peculiar place, so I've heard.'

All this made the children feel excited. Also Julian and Dick had always liked Sooty Lenoir. He was quite mad, but awfully good fun. They might have a first-rate time with him.

'Well – would you like to go? Or would you rather go back to school for the holidays?' asked Uncle Quentin impatiently.

'Oh *no* – not back to school!' said everyone at once.

'I'd *love* to go to Smuggler's Top,' said Dick. 'It sounds a thrilling place. And I always liked old Sooty, especially since he sawed half through one of the legs of our form-master's chair. It gave way at once when Mr. Toms sat down!'

'H'm. I don't see that a trick like that is any reason for liking someone,' said Uncle Quentin, beginning to feel a little doubtful about Master Lenoir. 'Perhaps, on the whole, school would be best for you.'

Oh no, no!' cried everyone. 'Let's go to Smuggler's Top! Do, do let's!'

'Very well,' said Uncle Quentin, pleased at their eager-
ness to follow his plan. 'As a matter of fact, I have already
settled it. I telephoned a few minutes ago. Mr. Lenoir
was very kind about it all.'

'Can I take Timmy?' asked George, suddenly.

'No,' said her father. 'I'm afraid not. Mr. Lenoir doesn't
like dogs.'

'Then I shouldn't like *him*,' said George, sulkily. 'I
won't go without Timmy.'

'You'll have to go back to school, then,' said her father,
sharply. 'And take off that sulky expression, George. You
know how I dislike it.'

But George wouldn't. She turned away. The others
looked at her in dismay. Surely old George wasn't going
to get into one of her moods, and spoil everything! It
would be fun to go to Smuggler's Top. But, of course,
it certainly wouldn't be so much fun without Timmy.
Still – they couldn't all go back to school just because
George wouldn't go anywhere without her dog.

They all went into the sitting-room. Anne put her arm
through George's. George shook it off.

'George! You simply *must* come with us,' said Anne.
'I can't bear to go without you – it would be awful to see
you going back to school all alone.'

'I shouldn't be all alone,' said George. 'I should have
Timmy.'

The others pressed her to change her mind, but she
shook them off. 'Leave me alone,' she said. 'I want to
think. How are we supposed to get to Smuggler's Top, and
where is it? Which road do we take?'

'We're going by car, and it's right up the coast somewhere, so I expect we'll take the coast-road,' said Julian.
'Why, George?'

'Don't ask questions,' said George. She went out with

Timmy. The others didn't follow her. George was not very nice when she was cross.

Aunt Fanny began to pack for them, though it was impossible to get some of the things from the girls' room. After a time George came back, but Timmy was not with her. She looked more cheerful.

'Where's Tim?' asked Anne, at once.

'Out somewhere,' said George.

'Are you coming with us, George?' asked Julian, looking at her.

'Yes. I've made up my mind to,' said George, but for some reason she wouldn't look Julian in the eyes. He wondered why.

Aunt Fanny gave them all an early lunch, and then a big car came for them. They packed themselves inside. Uncle Quentin gave them all sorts of messages for Mr. Lenoir, and Aunt Fanny kissed them good-bye. 'I do hope you have a nice time at Smuggler's Top,' she said. 'Mind you write at once and tell me all about it.'

'Aren't we going to say good-bye to Timmy?' said Anne, her eyes opening wide in amazement at George forgetting. 'George, surely you're not going without saying good-bye to old Timmy!'

'Can't stop now,' said Uncle Quentin, afraid that George might suddenly become awkward again. 'Right, driver! You can go off now. Don't drive too fast, please.'

Waving and shouting the children drove away from Kirrin Cottage, sad when they looked back and saw the smashed roof under the fallen tree. Never mind – they had not been sent back to school. That was the main thing. Their spirits rose as they thought of Sooty and his queerly-named home, Smuggler's Top.

'Smuggler's Top! It sounds too exciting for words!' said Anne. 'I can picture it, an old house right on the top

of a hill. Fancy being an island once. I wonder why the sea went back and left marshes instead.'

George said nothing for a while, and the car speeded on. The others glanced at her once or twice, but came to the conclusion that she was grieving about Timmy. Still she didn't look very sad!

The car went over a hill and speeded down to the bottom. When they got there George leaned forward and touched the driver's arm.

'Would you stop a moment, please? We have to pick somebody up here.'

Julian, Dick and Anne stared at George in surprise. The driver, also rather surprised, drew the car to a standstill. George opened the car door and gave a loud whistle.

Something shot out of the hedge and hurled itself joyfully into the car. It was Timmy! He licked everyone, trod on everyone's toes, and gave the little short barks that showed he was excited and happy.

'Well,' said the driver, doubtfully, 'I don't know if you're supposed to take that dog in, Miss. Your father didn't say anything about him.'

'It's all right,' said George, her face red with joy. 'Quite all right. You needn't worry. Start the car again, please.'

'You *are* a monkey!' said Julian, half-annoyed with George, and half-pleased because Timmy was with them after all. 'Mr. Lenoir may send him back, you know.'

'Well, he'll have to send *me* back too,' said George, defiantly. 'Anyhow, the main thing is, we've got Timmy after all, and I am coming with you.'

'Yes – that's fine,' said Anne, and gave first George and then Timmy a hug. '*I* didn't like going without Tim either.'

'On to Smuggler's Top!' said Dick, as the car started off again. 'On to Smuggler's Top. I wonder if we shall have any adventures there!'

SMUGGLER'S TOP

THE car sped on, mostly along the coast, though it sometimes went inland for a few miles. But sooner or later it was in sight of the sea again. The children enjoyed the long drive. They were to stop somewhere for lunch, and the driver told them he knew of a good inn.

At half past twelve he drew up outside an old inn, and they all trooped in. Julian took charge, and ordered lunch. It was a very good one, and all the children enjoyed it. So did Timmy. The innkeeper liked dogs, and put down such a piled-up plate for Timmy that the dog hardly liked to begin on his meal in case it was not for him!

He looked up at George and she nodded to him. 'It's your dinner, Timmy. Eat it up.'

So he ate it, hoping that if they were going to stay anywhere they might be staying at the inn. Meals like this did not arrive every day for a hungry dog!

But after lunch the children got up. They went to find the driver, who was having his lunch in the kitchen with the innkeeper and his wife. They were old friends of his.

'Well, I hear you're going to Castaway,' said the innkeeper, getting up. 'You be careful there!'

'Castaway!' said Julian. 'Is that what the hill is called, where Smuggler's Top is?'

'That's its name,' said the innkeeper.

'Why is it called that?' said Anne. 'What a funny name! Were people cast away on it once, when it was an island?'

'Oh no. The old story goes that the hill was once joined to the mainland,' said the innkeeper. 'But it was the haunt of bad people, and one of the saints became angry with the place, and cast it away into the sea, where it became an island.'

'And so it was called Castaway,' said Dick. 'But perhaps it has got good again, because the sea has gone away from it, and you can walk from the mainland to the hill, can't you?'

'Yes. There's one good road you can take,' said the innkeeper. 'But you be careful of wandering away from it, if you go walking on it! The marsh will suck you down in no time if you set foot on it!'

'It does sound a most exciting place,' said George. 'Smuggler's Top on Castaway Hill! Only one road to it!'

'Time to get on,' said the driver, looking at the clock. 'You've got to be there before tea, your uncle said.'

They got into the car again, Timmy clambering over legs and feet to a comfortable place on George's lap. He was far too big and heavy to lie there but just occasionally he seemed to want to, and George never had the heart to refuse him.

They drove off once more. Anne fell asleep, and the others felt drowsy too. The car purred on and on. It began to rain, and the countryside looked rather dreary.

The driver turned round after a while and spoke to Julian. 'We're coming near to Castaway Hill, sir. We'll soon be leaving the mainland, and taking the road across the marsh.'

Julian woke Anne. They all sat up expectantly. But it was very disappointing after all! The marshes were full of mist! The children could not pierce through it with their eyes, and could only see the flat road they were on, raised a little higher than the surrounding flat marsh.

When the mist shifted a little now and again the children saw a dreary space of flat marsh on either side.

'Stop a minute, driver,' said Julian. 'I'd like to see what the marsh is like.'

'Well, don't step off the road,' warned the driver, stopping the car. 'And don't you let that dog out, Miss. Once he runs off the road and gets into the marsh he'll be gone for good.'

'What do you mean – gone for good?' said Anne, her eyes wide.

'He means the marsh will suck down Timmy at once,' said Julian. 'Shut him in the car, George.'

So Timmy, much to his disgust, was shut safely in the car. He pawed at the door, and tried to look out of the window. The driver turned and spoke to him. 'It's all right. They'll be back soon old fellow!'

But Timmy whined all the time the others were out of the car. He saw them go to the edge of the road. He saw Julian jump down the couple of feet that raised the road above the marsh.

There was a line of raised stones running in the marsh alongside the road. Julian stood on one of these peering at the flat marsh.

'It's mud,' he said. 'Loose, squelchy mud! Look, when I touch it with my foot it moves! It would soon suck me down if I trod heavily on it.'

Anne didn't like it. She called to Julian. 'Come up on the road again. I'm afraid you'll fall in.'

Mists were wreathing and swirling over the salty marshes. It was a weird place, cold and damp. None of the children liked it. Timmy began to bark in the car.

'Tim will scratch the car to bits if we don't get back,' said George. So they all went back, rather silent. Julian wondered how many travellers had been lost in that strange sea-marsh.

'Oh, there's many that's never been heard of again,' said the driver, when they asked him. 'They do say there's one or two winding paths that go to the hill from the mainland, that were used before the road was built. But unless you know every inch of them you're off them in a trice, and find your feet sinking in the mud.'

'It's horrid to think about,' said Anne. 'Don't let's talk about it any more. Can we see Castaway Hill yet?'

'Yes. There it is, looming up in the mist,' said the driver. 'The top of it is out of the mist, see? Queer place, isn't it?'

The children looked in silence. Out of the slowly moving mists rose a tall, steep hill, whose rocky sides were as steep as cliffs. The hill seemed to swim in the mists, and to have no roots in the earth. It was covered with buildings which even at that distance looked old and quaint. Some of them had towers.

'That must be Smuggler's Top, right at the summit,' said Julian, pointing. 'It's like an old building of centuries ago – probably is! Look at the tower it has. What a wonderful view you'd get from it.'

The children gazed at the place where they were to stay. It looked exciting and picturesque, certainly – but it also looked rather forbidding.

'It's sort of – sort of *secret,* somehow,' said Anne, putting into words what the others were thinking. 'I mean – it looks as if it had kept all kinds of queer secrets down the centuries. I guess it could tell plenty of tales!'

The car drove on again, quite slowly, because the mists came down thickly. The road had a line of sparkling round buttons set all along the middle, and when the driver switched on his fog-lamp, they shone brightly and guided

him well. Then as they neared Castaway Hill the road began to slope upwards.

'We go through a big archway soon,' said the driver.
'That used to be where the city gate once was. The
whole town is surrounded by wall still, just as it used to
be in olden times. It's wide enough to walk on, and if you
start at a certain place, and walk long enough, you'll
come round to the place you started at!'

All the children made up their minds to do this without fail. What a view they would have all round the hill,
if they chose a fine day!

The road became steeper, and the driver put the en-
gine into a lower gear. It groaned up the hill. Then it
came to an archway, from which old gates were fastened
back. It passed through, and the children were in Castaway.

'It's almost as if we've gone back through the centuries,
and come to somewhere that existed ages ago!' said
Julian, peering at the old houses and shops, with their
cobbled streets, their diamond-paned windows, and stout
old doors.

They went up the winding high street, and came at
last to a big gateway, set with wrought-iron gates. The
driver hooted and they opened. They swept into a steep
drive, and at last stopped before Smuggler's Top.

They got out, feeling suddenly shy. The big old house
seemed to frown down at them. It was built of brick and
timber, and its front door was as massive as that of a
castle.

Queer gables jutted here and there over the diamond-
paned windows. The house's one tower stood sturdily
at the east side of the house, with windows all round. It
was not a square tower, but a rounded one, and ended in
a point.

'Smuggler's Top!' said Julian. 'It's a good name for it somehow. I suppose lots of smuggling went on here in the old days.'

Dick rang the bell. To do this he had to pull down an iron handle, and a jangling at once made itself heard in the house.

There was the sound of running feet, and the door was opened. It opened slowly, for it was heavy.

Beyond it stood two children, one a girl of about Anne's age, and the other a boy of Dick's age.

'Here you are at last!' cried the boy, his dark eyes dancing. 'I thought you were never coming!'

'This is Sooty,' said Dick to the girls, who had not met him before. They stared at him.

He was certainly very very dark. Black hair, black eyes, black eyebrows, and a brown face. In contrast to him the girl beside him looked pale and delicate. She had golden hair, blue eyes and her eyebrows were so faint they could hardly be seen.

'This is Marybelle, my sister,' said Sooty. 'I always think we look like Beauty and the Beast!'

Sooty was nice. Everyone liked him at once. George found herself twinkling at him in a way quite strange to her, for usually she was shy of strangers, and would not make friends for some time. But who could help liking Sooty with his dancing black eyes and his really wicked grin?

'Come in,' said Sooty. 'Driver, you can take the car round to the next door, and Block will take in the luggage for you and give you tea.'

Suddenly Sooty's face lost its smile and grew very solemn. He had seen Timmy!

'I say! I say – that's not your dog, is it?' he said.

'He's mine,' said George, and she laid a protecting hand

on Timmy's head. 'I had to bring him. I can't go anywhere without him.'

'Yes, but — no dog's allowed at Smuggler's Top,' said
Sooty, still looking very worried, and glancing behind
him as if he was afraid someone might come along and
see Timmy. 'My stepfather won't allow any dogs here.
Once I brought in a stray one and he licked me till
I couldn't sit down — my stepfather licked me, I mean, not
the dog.'

Anne gave a frightened little smile at the poor joke.
George looked stubborn and sulky.

'I thought — I thought maybe we could hide him somewhere while we were here,' she said. 'But if that's how
you feel, I'll go back home with the car. Good-bye.'

She turned and went after the car, which was backing
away. Timmy went with her. Sooty stared, and then he
yelled after her. 'Come back, stupid! We'll think of *some-*
thing!'

Chapter Five

SOOTY LENOIR

Sooty ran down the steps that led to the front door, and tore after George. The others followed. Marybelle went too, shutting the big front door behind her carefully.

There was a small door in the wall just where George was. Sooty caught hold of her and pushed her roughly through the door, holding it open for the others.

'Don't shove me like that,' began George, angrily. 'Timmy will bite you if you push me about.'

'No, he won't,' said Sooty, with a cheerful grin. 'Dogs like me. Even if I boxed your ears your dog would only wag his tail at me.'

The children found themselves in a dark passage. There was a door at the farther end. 'Wait here a minute and I'll see if the coast is clear,' said Sooty. 'I know my step-father is in, and I tell you, if he sees that dog he'll pack you all into the car again, and send you back! And I don't want him to do that because I can't tell you how I've looked forward to having you all!'

He grinned at them, and their hearts warmed towards him again, even George's, though she still felt angry at being so roughly pushed. She kept Timmy close beside her.

All the same everyone felt a bit scared of Mr. Lenoir. He sounded rather a fierce sort of person!

Sooty tiptoed to the door at the end of the passage and opened it. He peeped into the room there, and then came back to the others.

'All clear,' he said. 'We'll take the secret passage to my

bedroom. No one will see us then, and once we're there we can make plans to hide the dog. Ready?'

A secret passage sounded thrilling. Feeling rather as if they were in an adventure story, the children went quietly to the door and into the room beyond. It was a dark, oak-panelled room, evidently a study of some sort, for there was a big desk there, and the walls were lined with books. There was no one there.

Sooty went to one of the oak panels in the wall, felt along it deftly, and pressed in a certain place. The panel slid softly aside. Sooty put in his hand and pulled at something. A much larger panel below slid into the wall, and left an opening big enough for the children to pass through.

'Come on,' said Sooty in a low voice. 'Don't make a row.'

Feeling excited, the children all passed through the opening. Sooty came last, and did something that shut the opening and slid the first panel back into its place again.

He switched on a small torch, for it was pitch dark where the children were standing.

They were in a narrow stone passage, so narrow that two people could not possibly have passed one another unless both were as thin as rakes. Sooty passed his torch along to Julian, who was in front.

'Keep straight on till you come to stone steps,' he said. 'Go up them, turn to the right at the top, and keep straight on till you come to a blank wall, then I'll tell you what to do.'

Julian led the way, holding up the torch for the others. The narrow passage ran straight, and came to some stone steps. It was not only very narrow but rather low, so that Anne and Marybelle were the only ones who did not have to bend their heads.

Anne didn't like it very much. She never liked being in a very narrow enclosed space. It reminded her of dreams she sometimes had of being somewhere she couldn't get away from. She was glad when Julian spoke. 'The steps are here. Up we go, everyone.'

'Don't make a row,' said Sooty, in a low voice. 'We're passing the dining-room now. There's a way into this passage from there too.'

Everyone fell silent, and tried to walk on tiptoe, though this was unexpectedly difficult when heads had to be bent and shoulders stooped.

They climbed up fourteen steps, which were quite steep, and curved round half-way. Julian turned to the right at the top. The passage ran upwards then, and was as narrow as before. Julian felt certain that a very fat person could not possibly get along it.

He went on until, with a start, he almost bumped into a blank stone wall! He flashed his torch up and down it. A low voice came from the back of the line of children.

'You've got to the blank wall, Julian. Shine your torch up to where the roof of the passage meets the wall. You will see an iron handle there. Press down on it hard.'

Julian flashed his torch up and saw the handle. He put his torch into his left hand, and grasped the thick iron handle with his right. He pressed down as hard as he could.

And, quite silently, the great stone in the middle of the wall slid forward and sideways, leaving a gaping hole.

Julian was astonished. He let go the iron handle and flashed his torch into the hole. There was nothing but darkness there!

'It's all right It leads into a big cupboard in my bed-room!' called Sooty from the back. 'Get through, Julian, and we'll follow. There won't be anyone in my room.'

Julian crawled through the hole and found himself in a spacious cupboard, hung with Sooty's clothes. He groped his way through them and bumped against a door. He opened it and at once daylight flooded into the cupboard, lighting up the way from the passage into the room.

One by one the others clambered through the hole, lost themselves in clothes for a moment and then went thankfully into the room through the cupboard door.

Timmy, puzzled and silent, followed close beside George. He had not liked the dark, narrow passage very much. He was glad to be in daylight again!

Sooty, coming last, carefully closed the opening into the passage by pressing the stone back. It worked easily, though Julian could not imagine how. There must be some sort of pivot, he thought.

Sooty joined the others in his bedroom, grinning. George had her hand on Timmy's collar. 'It's all right, George,' said Sooty. 'We're quite safe here. My room and Marybelle's are separate from the rest of the house. We're in a wing on our own, reached by a long passage!'

He opened the door and showed the others what he meant. There was a room next to his, which was Marybelle's. Beyond stretched a stone-floored, stone-walled passage, laid with mats. At the end of it a big window let in light. There was a door there, a great oak one, which was shut.

'See? We're quite safe here, all by ourselves,' said Sooty. 'Timmy could bark if he liked, and no one would know.'

'But doesn't anyone ever come?' said Anne, surprised. 'Who keeps your rooms tidy, and cleans them?'

'Oh, Sarah comes and does that every morning,' said Sooty. 'But usually no one else comes. And anyway, I've got a way of knowing when anyone opens that door!'

He pointed to the door at the end of the passage. The others stared at him.

'How *do* you know?' said Dick.

'I've rigged up something that makes a buzzing noise here, in my room, as soon as that door is opened,' said Sooty, proudly. 'Look, I'll go along and open it, while you stay here and listen.'

He sped along the passage and opened the heavy door at the end. Immediately a low buzzing noise sounded somewhere in his room, and made everyone jump. Timmy was startled too, pricked up his ears, and growled fiercely.

Sooty shut the door and ran back. 'Did you hear the noise? It's a good idea, isn't it? I'm always thinking of things like that.'

The others thought they had come to rather a queer place! They stared round Sooty's bedroom, which was quite ordinary in its furnishings, and in its general untidiness. There was a big diamond-paned window, and Anne went to look out of it.

She gave a gasp. She had not expected to look down such a precipice! Smuggler's Top was built at the summit of the hill, and, on the side where Sooty's bedroom was, the hill fell away steeply, down and down to the marsh below!

'Oh look!' she said. 'Look how steep it is! It really gives me a very queer feeling to look down there!'

The others crowded round and looked in silence, for it certainly was strange to gaze down such a long way.

The sun was shining up on the hill-summit, but all around, as far as they could see, mists hid the marsh and the far-off sea. The only bit of the marsh that could be seen was far down below, at the bottom of the steep hill.

'When the mists are away, you can see over the flat marshes to where the sea begins,' said Sooty. 'That's quite a fine sight. You can hardly tell where the marsh ends and sea begins except when the sea is very blue. Fancy, once upon a time, the sea came right up and around this hill, and it was an island.'

'Yes. The innkeeper told us that,' said George. 'Why did the sea go back and leave it?'

'I don't know,' said Sooty. 'People say it's going back farther and farther. There's a big scheme on foot to drain the marsh, and turn it into fields, but I don't know if that will ever happen.'

'I don't like that marsh,' said Anne, with a shiver. 'It looks wicked, somehow.'

Timmy whined. George remembered that they must hide him, and make plans for him. She turned to Sooty.

'Did you mean what you said about hiding Tim?' she asked. 'Where shall we put him? And can he be fed? And how can we exercise him? He's a big dog, you know.'

'We'll plan it all,' said Sooty. 'Don't you worry. I love dogs, and I shall be thrilled to have Timmy here. But I do warn you that if my stepfather ever finds out we shall probably all get a jolly good thrashing, and you'll be sent home in disgrace.'

'But why doesn't your father like dogs?' said Anne puzzled. 'Is he afraid of them?'

'No, I don't think so. It's just that he won't have them here in the house,' said Sooty. 'I think he must have a reason for it, but I don't know what it is. He's a queer sort of man, my stepfather!'

'How is he queer?' asked Dick.

'Well — he seems full of secrets,' said Sooty. 'Queer people come here, and they come secretly without anyone knowing. I've seen lights shining in our tower on certain nights, but I don't know who puts them there or why. I've tried to find out, but I can't.'

'Do you think — do you think your father is a smuggler?' said Anne, suddenly.

'I don't think so,' said Sooty. 'We've got one smuggler here, and everyone knows him! See that house over there to the right, lower down the hill? Well, that's where he lives. He's as rich as can be. His name is Barling. Even the police know his goings-on, but they can't stop him! He is very rich and very powerful, so he does what he likes — and he won't let anyone play the same game as he

plays! No one else would dare to do any smuggling in
Castaway, while *he* does it!'

'This seems rather an exciting place,' said Julian. 'I
have a kind of feeling there might be an adventure somewhere about!'

'Oh no,' said Sooty. 'Nothing ever happens, really. It's
only just a feeling you get here, because the place is so old,
so full of secret ways and pits and passages. Why, the
whole hill is mined with passages in the rock, used by the
smugglers of olden times!'

'Well,' began Julian, and stopped very suddenly.
Everyone stared at Sooty. His secret buzzer had suddenly
barked from its hidden corner! Someone had opened the
door at the end of the passage!

Chapter Six

SOOTY'S STEPFATHER AND MOTHER

'SOMEONE'S coming!' said George, in a panic. 'What shall we do with Tim? Quick!'

Sooty took Timmy by the collar and shoved him into the old cupboard, and shut the door on him. 'Keep quiet!' he commanded, and Timmy stood still in the darkness, the hairs at the back of his neck standing up, his ears cocked.

'Well,' began Sooty, in a bright voice, 'perhaps I'd better show you where your bedrooms are now!'

The door opened and a man came in. He was dressed in black trousers and a white linen coat. He had a queer face. 'It's a shut face,' thought Anne to herself. 'You can't tell a bit what he's like inside, because his face is all shut and secret.'

'Oh hallo, Block,' said Sooty, airily. He turned to the others. 'This is Block, my stepfather's man,' he said. 'He's deaf, so you can say what you like, but it's better not to, because though he doesn't hear he seems to sense what we say.'

'Anyway, I think it would be beastly to say things we wouldn't say in front of him if he wasn't deaf,' said George, who had very strict ideas about things of that sort.

Block spoke in a curiously monotonous voice. 'Your stepfather and your mother want to know why you have not brought your friends to see them,' he said. 'Why did you rush up here like this?'

Block looked all round as he spoke – almost as if he knew there was a dog, and wondered where he had gone

47

to, George thought, in alarm. She did hope the car-driver had not mentioned Timmy.

'Oh – I was so pleased to see them I took them straight up here!' said Sooty. 'All right, Block. We'll be down in a minute.'

The man went, his face quite impassive. Not a smile, not a frown! 'I don't like him,' said Anne. 'Has he been with you long?'

'No – only about a year,' said Sooty. 'He suddenly appeared one day. Even Mother didn't know he was coming! He just came, and, without a word, changed into that white linen coat, and went to do some work in my stepfather's room. I suppose my stepfather was expecting him – but he didn't say anything to my mother, I'm sure of that. She seemed so surprised.

'Is she your real mother, or a stepmother, too?' asked Anne.

'You don't have a stepmother *and* a stepfather!' said Sooty, scornfully. 'You only have one or the other. My mother is my real mother, and she's Marybelle's mother, too. But Marybelle and I are only half-brother and sister, because my stepfather is her *real* father.'

'It's rather muddled,' said Anne, trying to sort it out.

'Come on – we'd better go down,' said Sooty, remembering. 'By the way, my stepfather is always being very affable, always smiling and joking – but it isn't real, somehow. He's quite likely to fly into a furious temper at any moment.'

'I hope we shan't see very much of him,' said Anne, uncomfortably. 'What's your mother like, Sooty?'

'Like a frightened mouse!' said Sooty. 'You'll like her, all right. She's a darling. But she doesn't like living here; she doesn't like this house, and she's terrified of my stepfather. She wouldn't say so herself, of course, but I know she is.'

Marybelle, who was too shy to have joined in any talking until then, nodded her head.

'I don't like living here, either,' she said. 'I shall be glad when I go to boarding-school, like Sooty. Except that I shall leave Mother all alone then.'

'Come on,' said Sooty, and led the way. 'We'd better leave Timmy in the cupboard till we come back, just in case Block does a bit of snooping. I'll lock the cupboard door and take the key.'

Feeling rather unhappy at leaving Timmy locked up in the cupboard, the children followed Sooty and Marybelle down the stone passage to the oak door. They went through, and found themselves at the top of a great flight of stairs, wide and shallow. They went down into a big hall.

At the right was a door, and Sooty opened it. He went in and spoke to someone.

'Here they all are,' he said. 'Sorry I rushed them off to my bedroom like that, Father, but I was so excited to see them all!'

'Your manners still need a little polishing, Pierre,' said Mr. Lenoir, in a deep voice. The children looked at him. He sat in a big oak chair, a neat, clever-looking man, with fair hair brushed upwards, and eyes as blue as Marybelle's. He smiled all the time, but with his mouth, not his eyes.

'What cold eyes!' thought Anne, when she went forward to shake hands with him. His hand was cold, too. He smiled at her, and patted her on the shoulder.

'What a nice little girl!' he said. 'You will be a good companion for Marybelle. Three boys for Sooty, and one girl for Marybelle. Ha ha!'

He evidently thought George was a boy, and she did
look rather like one – she was wearing shorts and jersey,
as usual, and her curly hair was very short.

Nobody said that George wasn't a boy. Certainly
George was not going to! She, Dick and Julian shook
hands with Mr. Lenoir. They had not even noticed
Sooty's mother!

She was there, though, sitting lost in an arm-chair, a
tiny woman like a doll, with mouse-coloured hair and
grey eyes. Anne turned to her.

'Oh, how small you are!' she said, before she could
stop herself.

Mr. Lenoir laughed. He laughed no matter what anyone said. Mrs. Lenoir got up and smiled. She was only
as tall as Anne, and had the smallest hands and feet that
Anne had ever seen on a grown-up. Anne liked her. She
shook hands, and said, 'It's so nice of you to have us all
here like this. You know, I expect, that a tree fell on the
roof of our house and smashed it.'

Mr. Lenoir's laugh came again. He made some kind of
joke, and everyone smiled politely.

'Well, I hope you'll have a good time here,' he said.
'Pierre and Marybelle will show you the old town, and, if
you promise to be careful, you can walk along the road to
the mainland to go to the cinema there.'

'Thank you,' said everyone, and Mr. Lenoir laughed
his curious laugh again.

'Your father is a very clever man,' he said, suddenly
turning to Julian, who guessed that he had mistaken him
for George. 'I am hoping he will come here to fetch you
home again when you go, and then I shall have the
pleasure of talking with him. He and I have been doing
the same kind of experiments, but he has got further than
I have.'

'Oh!' said Julian, politely. Then the doll-like Mrs.
Lenoir spoke in her soft voice.

'Block will give you all your meals in Marybelle's schoolroom, then you will not disturb my husband. He does not
like talk at meal-times, and that would be rather hard on
six children.'

Mr. Lenoir laughed again. His cold blue eyes looked
intently at all the children. 'By the way, Pierre,' he said
suddenly, 'I forbid you to wander about the catacombs
in this hill, as I have forbidden you before, and I also forbid you to do any of your dare-devil climbing, nor will I
have you acting about on the city wall, now that you have

others here. I will not have them taking risks. Will you promise me this?'

'I don't act about on the city wall,' protested Sooty. 'I don't take risks, either.'

'You play the fool always,' said Mr. Lenoir, and the tip of his nose turned quite white. Anne looked at it with interest. She did not know that it always did this when Mr. Lenoir got angry.

'Oh, sir – I was top of my form last term,' said Sooty, in a most injured tone. The others felt certain that he was trying to lead Mr. Lenoir away from his request – he was not going to promise him what he had asked!

Mrs. Lenoir now joined in. 'He really did do well last term,' she said. 'You must remember –'

'Enough!' snapped Mr. Lenoir, and the smiles and laughs he had so freely lavished on everyone vanished, entirely. 'Get out, all of you!'

Rather scared, Julian, Dick, Anne and George hurried from the room, followed by Marybelle and Sooty. Sooty was grinning as he shut the door.

'I didn't promise!' he said. 'He wanted to take all our fun away. This place isn't any fun if you don't explore it. I can show you heaps of queer places.'

'What are catacombs?' asked Anne, with a vague picture of cats and combs in her head.

'Winding, secret tunnels in the hill,' said Sooty. 'Nobody knows them all. You can get lost in them easily, and never get out again. Lots of people have.'

'Why are there so many secret ways and things here?' wondered George.

'Easy!' said Julian. 'It was a haunt of smugglers, and there must have been many a time when they had to hide not only their goods, but themselves! And, according to old Sooty, there still *is* a smuggler here!'

What did you say his name was – Barling, wasn't it?'

'Yes,' said Sooty. 'Come on upstairs and I'll show you your rooms. You've got a good view over the town.'

He took them to two rooms set side by side, on the opposite side of the big staircase from his bedroom and Marybelle's. They were small but well-furnished, and had, as Sooty said, a marvellous view over the quaint roofs and towers of Castaway Hill. They also had a remarkably good view of Mr. Barling's house.

George and Anne were to sleep in one room, and Julian and Dick in the other. Evidently Mrs. Lenoir had taken the trouble to remember that there were two girls and two boys, not one girl and three boys, as Mr. Lenoir imagined!

'Nice cosy rooms,' said Anne. 'I like these dark oak panels. Are there any secret passages in our rooms, Sooty?'

'You wait and see!' grinned Sooty. 'Look, there are your things, all unpacked from your suitcases. I expect Sarah did that. You'll like Sarah. She's a good sort, fat and round and jolly – not a bit like Block!'

Sooty seemed to have forgotten all about Tim. George reminded him.

'What about Timmy? He'll have to be near me, you know. And we must arrange to feed him and exercise him. Oh, I do hope he'll be all right, Sooty, I'd rather leave straight away than have Timmy unhappy.'

'He'll be all right!' said Sooty. 'I'll give him the free run of that narrow passage we came up to my bedroom by, and we'll feed him every chance we get. And we'll smuggle him out by a secret tunnel that opens half-way down the town, and give him plenty of exercise each morning. Oh, we'll have a grand time with Timmy!'

George wasn't so sure. 'Can he sleep with me at night?' she asked. 'He'll howl the place down if he can't.'

'Well – we'll try and manage it,' said Sooty, rather doubtfully. 'You've got to be jolly careful, you know. We don't want to land in serious trouble. You don't know what my stepfather can be like!'

They could guess, though. Julian looked curiously at Sooty. 'Was your own father's name Lenoir, too?' he asked.

Sooty nodded. 'Yes. He was my stepfather's cousin, and was as dark as all the Lenoirs usually are. My stepfather is an exception – he's fair. People say the fair Lenoirs are no good – but don't tell my stepfather that!'

'As if we should!' said George. 'Gracious, he'd cut off our heads or something! Come on – let's go back to Tim.'

Chapter Seven

THE HIDDEN PIT

THE children were all very glad to think that they were going to have meals by themselves in the old schoolroom. Nobody wanted to have much to do with Mr. Lenoir! They felt sorry for Marybelle because she had such a queer father.

They soon settled down at Smuggler's Top. Once George was satisfied that Timmy was safe and happy, though rather puzzled about everything, she settled down too. The only difficulty was getting Timmy to her room at night. This had to be done in darkness. Block had a most tiresome way of appearing silently and suddenly, and George was terrified of him catching a glimpse of the big dog.

Timmy had a queer sort of life the next few days! Whilst the children were indoors, he had to stay in the narrow secret passage, where he wandered about, puzzled and lonely, pricking his ears for a sound of the whistle that meant he was to come to the cupboard and be let out.

He was fed very well, for Sooty raided the larder every night. Sarah, the cook, was amazed at the way things like soup-bones disappeared. She could not understand it. But Timmy devoured everything that was given to him.

Each morning he was given good exercise by the children. The first morning this had been really very exciting!

George had reminded Sooty of his promise to take

55

Timmy for walks each day. 'He simply must have exercise, or he'll be terribly miserable!' she said. 'But how can we manage it? We can't possibly take him through the house and out of the front door! We'd be certain to walk into your father!'

'I told you I knew a way that came out half-way down the hill, silly,' said Sooty. 'I'll show you. We shall be quite safe once we are down there, because even if we met Block or anyone else that knew us, they wouldn't know it was our dog. They would think it was just a stray we had picked up.'

'Well — show us the way,' said George, impatiently. They were all in Sooty's bedroom, and Timmy was lying on the mat beside George. They felt really safe in Sooty's room because of the buzzer that warned them when anyone opened the door at the end of the long passage.

'We'll have to go into Marybelle's room,' said Sooty. 'You'll get a shock when you see the way that leads down the hill, I can tell you!'

He looked out of the door. The door at the end of the passage was shut. 'Marybelle, slip along and peep through the passage door,' said Sooty. 'Warn us if anyone is coming up the stairs. If not, we'll all slip quickly into your room.'

Marybelle ran to the door at the end of the passage. She opened it, and at once the warning buzzer sounded in Sooty's room, making Timmy growl fiercely. Marybelle looked through the doorway to the stairs. Then she signalled to the others that no one was coming.

They all rushed out of Sooty's room into Marybelle's, and Marybelle came to join them. She was a funny little mouse of a girl, shy and timid. Anne liked her, and once or twice teased her for being so shy.

But Marybelle did not like being teased. Her eyes filled

with tears at once, and she turned away. 'She'll be better when she goes to school,' Sooty said. 'She can't help being shy, shut up all the year round in this queer house. She hardly ever sees anyone of her own age.'

They crowded into the little girl's bedroom and shut the door. Sooty turned the key in the lock. 'Just in case friend Block comes snooping,' he said with a grin.

Sooty began to move the furniture in the room to the sides, near the walls. The others watched in surprise and then helped. 'What's the idea of the furniture removal?' asked Dick, struggling with a heavy chest.

'Got to get this heavy carpet up,' panted Sooty. 'It's put there to hide the trap-door below. At least, that's what I've always thought.'

Once the furniture stood by the walls, it was easy to drag up the heavy carpet. There was a felt lining under it too, and that had to be pulled aside as well. Then the children saw a trap-door, let flat into the floor, with a ring-handle to pull it up.

They felt excited. Another secret way! This house seemed full of them. Sooty pulled at the ring and the heavy door came up quite easily. The children peered down, but they could see nothing. It was pitch-dark.

'Are there steps down?' asked Julian, holding Anne back in case she fell.

'No,' said Sooty, reaching out for a big torch he had brought in with him. 'Look!'

He switched on his torch, and the children gave a gasp. The trap-door led down to a pit, far, far below!

'Why! It's miles below the foundations of the house, surely!' said Julian, surprised. 'It's just a hole down to a big pit. What's it for?'

'Oh, it was probably used to hide people – or to get rid of them!' said Sooty. 'Nice little place, isn't it? If you fell down there you'd land with an awful bump!'

'But – how in the world could we get Timmy down there – or get down ourselves?' said George. '*I'm* not going to fall down it, that's certain!'

Sooty laughed. 'You won't have to,' he said. 'Look here.' He opened a cupboard and reached up to a wide shelf. He pulled something down, and the children saw that it was a rope-ladder, fine but very strong.

'There you are! We can all get down by that,' he said.

'Timmy can't,' said George at once. 'He couldn't possibly climb up or down a ladder.'

'Oh, couldn't he?' said Sooty. 'He seems such a clever dog – I should have thought he could easily have done a thing like that.'

'Well, he can't,' said George, decidedly. 'That's a silly idea.'

'I know,' said Marybelle, suddenly, going red at her boldness in breaking in on the conversation. 'I think I know! We could get the laundry basket and shut Timmy in it. And we could tie it with ropes, and let him down – and pull him up the same way!'

The others stared at her. 'Now that really *is* a brainwave!' said Julian, warmly. 'Good for you, Marybelle. Timmy would be quite safe in a basket. But it would have to be a big one.'

'There's a very big one in the kitchen,' said Marybelle. 'It's never used except when we have lots of people to stay, like now. We could borrow it.'

'Oh *yes*!' said Sooty. 'Of course we could. I'll go and get it now.'

'But what excuse will you give?' shouted Julian after him. Sooty had already unlocked the door and shot out! He was a most impatient person, and could never put off anything for a single minute.

Sooty didn't answer. He sped down the passage. Julian locked the door after him. He didn't want anyone coming in and seeing the dragged-up carpet and the yawning hole!

Sooty was back in two minutes, carrying a very heavy wicker laundry basket on his head. He banged on the door, and Julian unlocked it.

'Good!' said Julian. 'How did you get it? Did any-one mind?'

'Didn't ask them,' grinned Sooty. 'Nobody there to ask. Block's with Father, and Sarah has gone out shopping. I can always put it back if any awkward questions are asked.'

The rope-ladder was shaken out down the hole. It slipped like an uncoiling snake, down and down, and reached the pit at the bottom. Then Timmy was fetched from Sooty's room. He came in wagging his tail overjoyed at being with everyone again. George hugged him.

'Darling Timmy! I hate you being hidden away like this. But never mind, we're all going out together this morning!'

'I'll go down first,' said Sooty. 'Then you'd better let Timmy down. I'll tie his basket round with this rope. It's nice and strong, and there's plenty to let down. Better tie the other end to the end of the bed, then when we come up again we can easily pull him up.'

Timmy was made to get inside the big basket and lie down. He was surprised and barked a little. But George put her hand over his mouth.

'Sh! You mustn't say a word, Timmy,' she said. 'I know all this is very astonishing. But never mind, you'll have a marvellous walk at the end of it.'

Timmy heard the word 'walk' and was glad. That was

what he wanted – a really nice long walk in the open air and sunshine!

He didn't at all like having the lid shut down on him, but as George seemed to think he must put up with all these queer happenings, Timmy did so, with a very good grace.

'He's really a marvellous dog,' said Marybelle. 'Sooty, get down the hole now, and be ready for when we let him down.'

Sooty disappeared down the dark hole, holding his torch between his teeth. Down and down he went, down and down. At last he stood safely at the bottom, and flashed his torch upwards. His voice came to them, sounding rather queer and far away.

'Come on! Lower Timmy down!'

The laundry basket, feeling extraordinarily heavy now, was pushed to the edge of the hole. Then down it went, knocking against the sides here and there. Timmy growled. He didn't like this game!

Dick and Julian had hold of the rope between them. They lowered Timmy as smoothly as they could. He reached the bottom with a slight bump, and Sooty undid the basket. Out leapt Timmy, barking! But his bark sounded very small and distant to the watchers at the top.

'Now come on down, one by one!' shouted up Sooty, waving his torch. 'Is the door locked, Julian?'

'Yes,' said Julian. 'Look out for Anne. She's coming now.'

Anne climbed down, a little frightened at first, but, as her feet grew use to searching for and finding the rungs of the rope-ladder, she went down quite quickly.

Then the others followed, and soon they were all standing together at the bottom of the hole, in the enormous pit. They looked round curiously. It had a musty smell,

and its walls were damp and greenish. Sooty swung his torch round, and the children saw various passages leading off here and there.

'Where do they all lead to?' asked Julian, in amazement.

'Well, I told you this hill was full of tunnels,' said Sooty. 'This pit is down in the hill and these tunnels lead into the catacombs. There are miles and miles of them. No one explores them now, because so many people have been lost in them and never heard of again. There used to be an old map of them, but it's lost.'

'It's weird!' said Anne, and shivered. 'I wouldn't like to be down here alone.'

'What a place to hide smuggled goods in,' said Dick. 'No one would ever find them here.'

'I guess the old-time smugglers knew every inch of these passages,' said Sooty. 'Come on! We'll take the one that leads out of the hillside. We'll have to do a bit of climbing when we get there. I hope you don't mind.'

'Not a bit,' said Julian. 'We're all good climbers. But I say, Sooty – you're sure you know the way? We don't want to be lost for ever down here!'

''Course I know the way! Come on!' said Sooty, and, flashing his torch in front of him, he led the way into a dark and narrow tunnel.

Chapter Eight

AN EXCITING WALK

THE tunnel ran slightly downwards, and smelt nasty in places. Sometimes it opened out into pits like the one they themselves had come from. Sooty flashed his torch up them.

'That one goes into Barling's house somewhere,' he said. 'Most of the old houses hereabouts have openings into pits, like ours. Jolly well hidden some of them are, too!'

'There's daylight or something in front!' said Anne, suddenly. 'Oh good! I hate this tunnel.'

Sure enough, it was daylight, creeping in through a kind of cave-entrance in the hillside. The children crowded there, and looked out.

They were outside the hill, and outside the town, somewhere on the steep cliff-side that ran down to the marsh. Sooty climbed out on to a ledge. He put his torch into his pocket.

'We've got to get to that path down there,' he said, pointing. 'That will lead us to a place where the city wall is fairly low, and we can climb over it. Is Timmy sure-footed? We don't want him tumbling into the marsh down there!'

The marsh lay a good way below, looking ugly and flat. George sincerely hoped Timmy would never fall into it. Still, he was very sure-footed, and she didn't think he would slip. The path was steep and rocky, but quite passable.

They all went down it, clambering over rocks now and again. The path led them to the city wall, which, as Sooty

had said, was fairly low just there. He climbed up to the top. He was like a cat for climbing!

'No wonder he's got such a name for climbing about everywhere at school!' said Dick to Julian. 'He's had good practice here. Do you remember how he climbed up to the roof of the school the term before last? Everyone was scared he'd slip and fall, but he didn't. He tied the Union Jack to one of the chimney-pots!'

'Come on!' called Sooty. 'The coast is clear. This is a lonely bit of the town, and no one will see us climbing up.'

Soon they were all over the wall, Timmy too. They set off for a good walk, swinging down the hill, enjoying themselves. The mist began to clear after a while, and the sun felt nice and warm.

The town was very old. Some of the houses seemed almost tumble-down, but there were people living in them, for smoke came from the chimneys. The shops were quaint, with their long narrow windows, and over-hanging eaves. The children stopped to look into them.

'Look out – here's Block!' said Sooty suddenly in a low voice. 'Don't take any notice of Timmy at all. If he comes around licking us or jumping up, pretend to try and drive him off as if he was a stray.'

They all pretended not to see Block, but gazed earnestly into the window of a shop. Timmy feeling rather out of it, ran up to George and pawed at her, trying to make her take notice of him.

'Go away, dog!' said Sooty, and flapped at the surprised Timmy. 'Go away! Following us about like this! Go home, can't you?'

Timmy thought this was some sort of a game. He barked happily, and ran round Sooty and George, giving them an occasional lick.

'Home, dog, home!' yelled Sooty, flapping hard again.

Then Block came up to them, no expression on his face at all. 'The dog bothers you?' he said. 'I will throw a stone at him and make him go.'

'Don't you dare!' said George, immediately. 'You go home yourself! I don't mind the dog following us. He's quite a nice one.'

'Block's deaf, silly,' said Sooty. 'It's no good talking to him.' To George's horror Block picked up a big stone, meaning to throw it at Timmy. George flew at him, punched him hard on the arm, and made him drop the stone.

'How dare you throw stones at a dog!' yelled the little girl in a fury. 'I'll – I'll tell the police.'

'Now, now,' said a voice nearby. 'What's all this about? Pierre, what's the trouble?'

The children turned and saw a tall man standing near them, wearing his hair rather long. He had long, narrow eyes, a long nose and a long chin. 'He's long everywhere!' thought Anne, looking at his long thin legs and long narrow feet.

'Oh, Mr. Barling! I didn't see you,' said Sooty, politely. 'Nothing's the matter, thanks. It's only that this dog is following us, and Block said he'd make it go away by chucking a stone at it. And George here is fond of dogs and got angry about that.'

'I see. And who are all these children?' said Mr. Barling, looking at each one of them out of his long, narrow eyes.

'They've come to stay with us because their uncle's house had an accident to it,' explained Sooty. 'George's father's house, I mean. At Kirrin.'

'Ah – at Kirrin?' said Mr. Barling, and seemed to prick up his long ears. 'Surely that is where that very clever scientist friend of Mr. Lenoir's lives?'

'Yes. He's my father,' said George. 'Why, do you know him?'

'I have heard of him – and of his very interesting experiments,' said Mr. Barling. 'Mr. Lenoir knows him well, I believe?'

'Not awfully well,' said George, puzzled. 'They just write to one another, I think. My father telephoned to Mr. Lenoir to ask him if he could have us to stay while our own house is being mended.'

'And Mr. Lenoir, of course, was only too delighted to have the whole company of you?' said Mr. Barling. '*Such* a good, generous fellow, your father, Pierre!'

The children stared at Mr. Barling, thinking that it was queer of him to say nice things in such a nasty voice.

They felt uncomfortable. It was plain that Mr. Barling did not like Mr. Lenoir at all. Well, neither did they, but they didn't like Mr. Barling any better!

Timmy saw another dog and darted happily after him. Block had now disappeared, going up the steep high street with his basket. The children said good-bye to Mr. Barling, not wanting to talk to him any more.

They went after Timmy, talking eagerly as soon as they had left Mr. Barling behind.

'Goodness – that was a narrow escape from Block!' said Julian. 'Old beast – going to throw that enormous stone at Timmy. No wonder you flew at him, George! You nearly gave the game away, though.'

'I don't care,' said George. 'I wasn't going to have Timmy's leg broken. It was a bit of bad luck meeting Block our very first morning out.'

'We'll probably never meet him again when we take Timmy out,' said Sooty, comfortingly. 'And if we do we'll simply say the dog always joins us when it meets us. Which is perfectly true.'

They enjoyed their walk. They went into a quaint old coffee shop and had steaming cups of delicious creamy coffee and jammy buns. Timmy had two of the buns and gobbled them greedily. George went off to buy some meat for him at the butcher's, choosing a shop that Sooty said Mrs. Lenoir did not go to. She did not want any butcher telling Mrs. Lenoir that the children had been buying dog-meat!

They went back the same way as they had come. They made their way up the steep cliff-path, and in at the tunnel-entrance, back through the winding tunnel to the pit, and there was the rope-ladder waiting for them. Julian and Dick went up first, while George packed the surprised Timmy into the basket again and tied the rope firmly round it. Then up went the whining Timmy, bumping against the sides of the hole, until the two panting boys pulled the basket into Marybelle's room and undid it.

It was ten minutes before the dinner-hour. 'Just time to shut the trap-door, pull back the carpet and wash our hands,' said Sooty. 'And I'll put old Timmy back into the secret passage behind the cupboard in my room, George. Where is that meat you bought? I'll put that in the passage too. He can eat it when he likes.'

'Did you put him a nice warm rug there, and a dish of fresh water?' asked George, anxiously, for the third or fourth time.

'You know I did. I keep telling you,' said Sooty. 'Look, we won't put back all the furniture except the chairs. We can say we want it left back because we like to play a game on the carpet. It'll be an awful bore if we have to move chests and things every time we exercise Tim.'

They were just in time for their dinner. Block was there to serve it, and so was Sarah. The children sat down hungrily, in spite of having had coffee and buns. Block and Sarah ladled out hot soup on to their plates.

'I hope you got rid of the unpleasant dog,' said Block in his monotonous voice. He gave George a rather nasty look. Evidently he had not forgotten how she had flown at him.

Sooty nodded. It was no good speaking in answer, for Block would not hear. Sarah bustled round, taking away the soup-plates and preparing to give them their second course.

The food was very good at Smuggler's Top. There was plenty of it, and the hungry visitors and Sooty ate everything put before them. Marybelle hadn't much appetite, but she was the only one. George tried to secrete tit-bits and bones whenever she could, for Timmy.

Two or three days went by, and the children fell into their new life quite happily. Timmy was taken out each morning for a long walk. The children soon got used to slipping down the rope-ladder, and making their way with Timmy to the cliff-side.

In the afternoons they went to either Sooty's room or Marybelle's, and played games or read. They could have Timmy there, because the buzzer always warned them if anyone was coming.

At night it was always an excitement to get Timmy to George's room without being seen. This was usually done when Mr. and Mrs. Lenoir were sitting at their dinner, and Block and Sarah were serving them. The children had a light supper first, and Mr. and Mrs. Lenoir had their dinner an hour later. It was quite the best time to smuggle Timmy along to George's room.

Timmy seemed to enjoy the smuggling. He ran silently beside George and Sooty, stopped at every corner, and scampered gladly into George's room as soon as he got there. He lay quietly under the bed till George was in bed herself, and then he came out to lie on her feet.

George always locked their door at night. She didn't want Sarah or Mrs. Lenoir coming in and finding Timmy there! But nobody came, and as night after night went by, George grew more easy about Timmy.

Taking him back to Sooty's room in the morning was a bit of nuisance, because it had to be done early, before anyone was up. But George could always wake herself at any time she chose, and each morning about half past six the little girl slipped through the house with Timmy. She went in at Sooty's door, and he jumped out of bed to deal with Timmy. He was always awakened by the buzzer that sounded when George opened the door at the end of the passage.

'I hope you are all enjoying yourselves,' Mr. Lenoir said to the children, whenever they met him in the hall or on the stairs. And they always replied politely. 'Oh yes, Mr. Lenoir, thank you.'

'It's quite a peaceful holiday after all,' said Julian. 'Nothing happens at all!'

And then things *did* begin to happen and once they had begun they never stopped!

Chapter Nine

WHO IS IN THE TOWER?

ONE night Julian was awakened by someone opening his door. He sat up at once. 'Who is it?' he said. 'Me, Sooty,' said Sooty's voice, very low. 'I say, I want you to come and see something.'

Julian woke Dick, and the two of them put on their dressing-gowns. Sooty led them quietly out of the room and took them to a queer little room, tucked away in an odd wing of the house. All kinds of things were kept here, trunks and boxes, old toys, chests of old clothes, broken vases that had never been mended, and many other worthless things.

'Look,' said Sooty, taking them to the window. They saw that the little room had a view of the tower belonging to the house. It was the only room in the house that did, for it was built at a queer angle.

The boys looked – and Julian gave an exclamation. Someone was signalling from the tower! A light there flashed every now and again. In and out – pause – flash, flash, in and out – pause. The light went regularly on and off in a certain rhythm.

'Now – who's doing that?' whispered Sooty.

'Your father?' wondered Julian.

'Don't think so,' said Sooty. 'I think I heard him snoring away in his room. We could go and find out though – see if he really is in his bedroom.'

'Well – for goodness sake don't let's get caught,' said Julian, not at all liking the idea of prying about in his host's house.

They made their way to where Mr. Lenoir had his room. It was quite plain he was there, for a regular low snoring came from behind the closed door.

'It may be Block up in the tower,' said Dick. 'He looks full of secrets. I wouldn't trust him an inch. I bet it's Block.'

'Well – shall we go to his room and see if it's empty?' whispered Sooty. 'Come on. If it's Block signalling, he's doing it without Father knowing.'

'Oh, your father might have told him to,' said Julian, who felt that he wouldn't trust Mr. Lenoir much further than he would trust Block.

They went up the back-stairs to the wing where the staff slept. Sarah slept in a room there with Harriet the kitchen-maid. Block slept alone.

Sooty pushed open Block's door very softly and slowly. When he had enough room to put in his head, he did so. The room was full of moonlight. By the window was Block's bed. And Block was there! Sooty could see the humpy shape of his body, and the black round patch that was his head.

He listened, but he could not catch Block's breathing. He must sleep very quietly.

He withdrew his head, and pushed the other two boys quietly down the back-stairs.

'Was he there?' whispered Julian.

'Yes. So it can't be him, signalling up in our tower,' said Sooty. 'Well – who can it be then? I don't like it. It couldn't possibly be Mother or Sarah or the little kitchen-maid. Is there a stranger in our house, someone we don't know, living here in secret?'

'Can't be!' said Julian, a little shiver running down his back. 'Look here – what about us going up to the tower and trying to peep through the door or something? We'd soon find out who it was then. Perhaps we ought to tell your father.'

'No. Not yet. I want to find out a whole lot more before I say anything to anyone,' said Sooty, sounding obstinate. 'Let's creep up to the tower. We shall have to be jolly careful though. You get to it by a spiral staircase, rather narrow. There's nowhere much to hide if anyone suddenly came down out of the tower.'

'What's in the tower?' whispered Dick, as they made their way through the dark and silent house, thin streaks of moonlight coming in here and there between the cracks of the closed curtains.

'Nothing much. Just a table and a chair or two, and a bookcase of books,' said Sooty. 'We use it on hot summer days when the breeze gets in strongly through the windows there, and we can see a long way all round us.'

They came to a little landing. From this a winding, narrow stairway of stone went up to the rounded tower. The boys looked up. Moonlight fell on the stairway from a slit-like window in the wall.

'We'd better not all go up,' said Sooty. 'We should find it so difficult to hurry down, three of us, if the person in the tower suddenly came out. I'll go. You stay down here and wait. I'll see if I can spy anything through the crack in the door or the key-hole.'

He crept softly up the stairway, soon lost to view as he rounded the first spiral. Julian and Dick waited in the shadows at the bottom. There was a thick curtain over one of the windows there, and they got behind it, wrapping its folds round them for warmth.

Sooty crept up to the top. The tower-room had a stout oak door, studded and barred. It was shut! It was no use trying to look through the crack, because there wasn't one. He bent down to peer through the key-hole.

But that was stuffed up with something, so he could not see through that either. He pressed his ear to it and listened.

He heard a series of little clicks. Click – click – click – click – click. Nothing else at all.

'That's the click of the light they're using,' thought Sooty. 'Still signalling like mad! What for? Who to? And who is in our tower-room, using it as a signalling-station? How I wish I knew!'

Suddenly the clicking stopped. There was the sound of someone walking across the stone floor of the tower. And almost at once the door opened!

Sooty had no time to hurry down the stairs. All he could do was to squeeze into a niche, and hope that the person would not see him or touch him as he went by. The moon went behind a cloud at that moment, and Sooty was thankful to know he was hidden in black shadow. Some-one came down the stairs and actually brushed against Sooty's arm.

Sooty jumped almost out of his skin, expecting to be hauled out of his niche. But the person did not seem to notice, and went on down the spiral stairway, walking softly.

Sooty did not dare to go down after him, for he was afraid the mon would come out, and cast his shadow down for the signaller to see.

So he stayed squeezed in his niche, hoping that Julian and Dick were well-hidden, and would not think it was he, Sooty, who was walking down the stairs!

Julian and Dick heard the soft footsteps coming, and thought at first it was Sooty. Then, not hearing his whis-per, they stiffened behind the curtains, guessing that it was the signaller himself who was walking by!

'We'd better follow him!' whispered Julian to Dick. 'Come on. Quiet, now!'

But Julian got muddled up with the great curtains, and could not seem to find his way out. Dick, however, slipped out easily enough, and padded after the disappearing person. The moon was now out again, and Dick could catch glimpses of the signaller as he went past the moonlight streaks. Keeping well in the shadows himself, he darted quietly after him. Where was he going?

He followed him across the landing to a passage. Then across another landing and up the back-stairs! But those led to the staff bedrooms. Surely the man was not going there?

Dick, to his enormous surprise, saw the person disappear silently into Block's bedroom. He crept to the door, which had been left a little ajar. There was no light in the room except that of the moon. There was no sound of talking. Nothing at all except a creak which might have come from the bed.

Dick peeped in, full of the most intense curiosity. Would he see the man waking up Block? Would he see him climbing out of the window?

He stared round the room. There was no one there at all, except Block lying in bed. The moonlight lit up the corners, and Dick could quite plainly see that the room was empty. Only Block lay there, and, as Dick watched, he heard him give a sigh and roll over in bed.

'Well! That's the queerest thing I ever saw,' thought Dick, puzzled. 'A man goes into a room and completely disappears, without a single sound! Where can he have gone?'

He went back to find the others. Sooty by this time had crept down the spiral staircase and had found Julian, who had explained that Dick had gone to follow the queer signaller.

They went to find Dick, and suddenly bumped into him, creeping along quietly in the darkness. They all jumped violently, and Julian almost cried out, but stifled his voice just in time.

'Golly! You gave me a scare, Dick!' he whispered. 'Well, did you see who it was and where he went?'

Dick told them of his queer experience. 'He simply went into Block's room and vanished,' he said. 'Is there any secret passage leading out of Block's room, Sooty?'

'No, none,' said Sooty. 'That wing is much newer than the rest of the house, and hasn't any secrets in at all. I simply can't imagine what happened to the man. How very queer! Who is he, and why does he come, and where on earth does he go?'

'We really must find out,' said Julian. 'It's such a mystery! Sooty, how did you know there was signalling going on from the tower?'

'Well, some time ago I found it out, quite by accident,' said Sooty. 'I couldn't sleep, and I went along to that funny little box-room place, and ferreted about for an old book I thought I'd seen there. And suddenly I looked up at the tower, and saw a light flashing there.'

'Funny,' said Dick.

'Well, I went along there at night a good many times after that, to see if I could see the signals again,' said Sooty, 'and at last I did. The first time I had seen them there was a good moon, and the second time there was, too. So, I thought, next time there's a moon, I'll creep along to that old box-room and see if the signaller is at work again. And sure enough he was!'

'Where does that window look out on, that we saw the light flashing from?' asked Julian, thoughtfully. 'The seaward side – or the landward?'

'Seaward,' said Sooty at once. 'There's something or someone out at sea that receives those signals. Goodness knows who.'

'Some kind of smugglers, I suppose,' said Dick. 'But it can't be anything to do with your father, Sooty. I say – let's go up into the tower, shall we? We might find something there – or see something.'

They went back to the spiral staircase and climbed up to the tower-room. It was dark, for the moon was behind a cloud. But it came out after a while, and the boys looked out of the seaward window.

There was no mist at all that night. They could see the flat marshes stretching away to the sea. They gazed down in silence. Then the moon went in and darkness covered the marsh.

Suddenly Julian clutched the others, making them jump. 'I can see something!' he whispered. 'Look beyond there. What is it?'

They all looked. It seemed like a tiny line of very small dots of light. They were so far away that it was difficult to see if they stayed still or moved. Then the moon came out again, flooding everywhere with silvery light, and the boys could not see anything except the moonshine.

But when the moon went in again, there was the line of tiny, pricking lights again! 'A bit nearer, surely!' whispered Sooty. 'Smugglers – coming over a secret path from the sea to Castaway Hill! Smugglers!'

Chapter Ten

TIMMY MAKES A NOISE

THE three girls were very excited the next day when the boys told them their adventure of the night before.

'Gracious!' said Anne, her eyes wide with surprise. 'Who can it be signalling like that? And wherever did he go to? Fancy him going into Block's room, with Block there in bed!'

'It's very peculiar,' said George. 'I wish you had come and told me and Anne.'

'There wasn't time – and anyway, we couldn't have Timmy about at night. He might have flown at the signaller,' said Dick.

'The man must have been signalling to the smugglers,' said Julian, thoughtfully. 'Let me see – probably they came over from France in a ship – came as near to the marsh as they could – waited for a signal to tell them that the coast was clear – probably the signal from the tower – and then waded across a path they knew through the marsh. Each man must have carried a torch to prevent himself from leaving the path and falling into the marsh. No doubt there was someone waiting to receive the goods they brought – someone at the edge of the marsh below the hill.'

'But who?' said Dick. 'It can't have been Mr. Barling, who, Sooty says, is known to be a smuggler. Because the signal lights came from *our* house, not his. It's all very puzzling.'

'Well, we'll do our best to solve the mystery,' said George. 'There's some queer game going on in this very house, with or without your father's knowledge, Sooty. We'll keep a jolly good lookout and see if we can find out what it is.'

They were at breakfast alone, when they discussed the night's adventure. Block came in to see if they had finished at that moment. Anne did not notice him.

'What does Mr. Barling smuggle?' she asked Sooty. Immediately she got a hard kick on her ankle, and stared in pain and surprise. 'Why did you . . .?' she began, and got another kick, harder still. Then she saw Block.

'But he's deaf,' she said. 'He can't hear anything we say.'

Block began to clear away, his face as usual showing no expression. Sooty glared at Anne. She was upset and cross, but said no more. She rubbed her bruised ankle hard. As soon as Block went out of the room she turned on Sooty.

'You mean thing! You hurt my ankle like anything! Why shouldn't I say things in front of Block? He's quite deaf!' said Anne, her face very red.

'I know he's supposed to be,' said Sooty. 'And I think he is. But I saw a funny look come over his face when you asked me what Mr. Barling smuggled – almost as if he had heard what you said, and was surprised.'

'You imagined it!' said Anne, crossly, still rubbing her ankle. 'Anyway, don't kick me so hard again. A gentle push with your toe would have been enough. I won't talk in front of Block if you don't want me to, but it's quite plain he's as deaf as a post!'

'Yes, he's deaf all right,' said Dick. 'I dropped a plate off the table yesterday, by accident, just behind him, and it smashed to bits, if you remember. Well, he didn't jump or turn a hair, as he would have done if he could have heard.'

'All the same – I never trust Block, deaf or not,' said Sooty. 'I always feel he might read our lips or something. Deaf people can often do that, you know.'

They went off to take Timmy for his usual morning walk. Timmy was quite used to being shut in the laundry basket by now, and lowered into the pit. In fact, he always jumped straight into the basket as soon as the lid was opened, and lay down.

That morning they again met Block, who stared with great interest at the dog. He plainly recognized it as the same dog as before.

'There's Block,' said Julian, in a low voice. 'Don't drive Timmy off this time. We'll pretend he's a stray who always meets us each morning.'

So they let Timmy run round them, and when Block came up, they nodded to him, and made as if to go on their way. But the man stopped them.

'That dog seems to be a friend of yours,' he said, in his curious monotone of a voice.

'Oh yes. He goes with us each morning now,' said Julian, politely. 'He quite thinks he's our dog! Nice fellow, isn't he?'

Block stared at Timmy, who growled. 'Mind you do not bring that dog into the house,' said Block. 'If you do, Mr. Lenoir will have him killed.'

Julian saw George's face beginning to turn red with fury. He spoke hurriedly. 'Why should we bring him to the house, Block? Don't be silly!'

Block, however, did not appear to hear. He gave Timmy a nasty look, and went on his way, occasionally turning round to look at the little company of children.

'Horrid fellow!' said George, angrily. 'How dare he say things like that?'

When they got back to Marybelle's bedroom that morning, they pulled Timmy up from the pit, and let him out of the basket. 'We'll put him into the secret passage as usual,' said George, 'and I'll put some biscuits in with him. I got some nice ones for him this morning, the sort he likes, all big and crunchy.'

She went to the door — but just as she was about to unlock it and take Timmy into Sooty's room next door, Timmy gave a small growl.

George took her hand away from the door at once. She turned to look at Timmy. He was standing stiffly, the hackles on his neck rising up, and he was staring fixedly at the door. George put her hand to her lips warningly, and whispered:

'Someone's outside. Timmy knows. He's smelt them. Will you all talk loudly, and pretend to be playing a game? I'll pop Timmy into the cupboard where the rope-ladder is kept.'

At once the others began to talk to one another, whilst George swiftly dragged Timmy to the cupboard, patted him to make him understand he was to be quiet, and shut him in.

'My turn to deal,' said Julian loudly, and took a pack of snap cards from the top of the chest. 'You won last time, Dick. Bet I'll win this time.'

He dealt swiftly. The others, still talking loudly, saying anything that came into their heads, began to play snap. They yelled 'snap' nearly all the time, pretending to be very jolly and hilarious. Anyone listening outside the door would never guess it was all pretence.

George, who was watching the door closely, saw that the handle was gradually turning, very slowly indeed. Someone meant to open the door without being heard, and come in unexpectedly. But the door was locked!

Soon the person outside, whoever it was, realized that

the door was locked, and the handle slowly turned the other way again. Then it was still. There came no other sound. It was impossible to know if anyone was still outside the door or not.

But Timmy would know! Signing to the others to carry on with their shouting and laughing, George let Timmy out of the cupboard. He ran to the door of the room, and stood there, sniffing quietly. Then he turned and looked at George, his tail wagging.

'It's all right,' said George to the others. 'There's no one there now. Timmy always knows. We'd better quickly take him into your room, Sooty, while the coast is clear. Who could it have been, do you think, snooping outside?'

'Block, I should say,' said Sooty. He unlocked the door and peered out. There was no one in the passage. Sooty tiptoed to the door at the end and looked out there also. He waved to George to tell her it was all right to take Timmy into his room.

Soon Timmy was safely in the secret passage, crunching up his favourite biscuits. He had got quite used to his queer life now, and did not mind at all. He knew his way about the passage, and had explored other passages that led from it. He was quite at home in the maze of secret ways!

'Better go and have our dinner now,' said Dick. 'And mind, Anne – don't go and say anything silly in front of that horrid Block, in case he reads your lips.'

'Of course I shan't,' said Anne, indignantly. 'I wouldn't have before, but I never thought of him reading my lips. If he does, he's very clever.'

Soon they were all sitting down to lunch. Block was there, waiting to serve them. Sarah was out for the day and did not appear. Block served them with soup, and then went out.

Suddenly, to the children's intense surprise and fright, they heard Timmy barking loudly! They all jumped violently.

'Listen! Hark at Timmy!' said Julian. 'He must be somewhere near here, in that secret passage. How weird it sounds, his bark coming muffled and distant like that. But anyone would know it was a dog barking.'

'Don't say anything at all about it in front of Block,' said Sooty. 'Not a word. Pretend not to hear at all, if Timmy barks again. What on earth is he barking for?'

'It's the bark he uses when he's excited and pleased,' said George. 'I expect he's chasing a rat. He always goes right off his head when he sees a rat or a rabbit. There he goes again. Oh, dear, I hope he catches the rat quickly and settles down!'

Block came back at that moment. Timmy had again just stopped barking. But, in a moment or two, his doggy voice could be heard once more, very muffled. 'Woof! Woof-woof!'

Julian was watching Block closely. The man went on serving the meat. He said nothing, but looked round at the children intently, as if he wanted to see each child's expression, or see if they said anything.

'Jolly good soup that was today,' said Julian, cheerfully, looking round at the others. 'I must say Sarah is a wonderful cook.'

'I think her ginger buns are gorgeous,' said Anne. 'Especially when they are all hot from the oven.'

'Woof-woof,' said Timmy's voice from far away behind the walls.

'George, your mother makes the most heavenly fruit cake I ever tasted,' said Dick to George, wishing Timmy would be quiet. 'I do wonder how they're all getting on

at Kirrin Cottage, and if they've started mending the roof yet.'

'Woof!' said Timmy, joyfully chasing his rat down another bit of passage.

Block served everyone and then silently disappeared. Julian went to the door to make sure he had gone and was not outside.

'I hope old Block *is* as deaf as a post!' he said. 'I could have sworn I saw a surprised look come into those cold eyes of his, when Timmy barked.'

'Well, if he *could* hear him, which I don't believe,' said George, 'he must have been jolly surprised to see us talking away and not paying any attention to a dog's barking at all!'

The others giggled. They kept a sharp ear for Block's return. They heard footsteps after a time, and began to pile their plates together for him to take away.

The schoolroom door opened. But it was not Block who came in. It was Mr. Lenoir! He came in, smiling as usual, and looked round at the surprised children.

'Ah! So you are enjoying your dinner, and eating it all up, like good children,' he said. He always irritated the children because he spoke to them as if they were very small. 'Does Block wait on you properly?'

'Oh yes, sir, thank you,' said Julian, standing up politely. 'We are having a very nice time here. We think Sarah is a wonderful cook!'

'Ah, that's good, that's good,' said Mr. Lenoir. The children waited impatiently for him to go. They were so afraid that Timmy would bark again. But Mr. Lenoir seemed in no hurry.

And then Timmy barked again! 'Woof, woof, woof!'

Chapter Eleven

GEORGE IS WORRIED

MR. LENOIR cocked his head on one side almost like a startled dog, when he heard the muffled barking. He looked at the children. But they made no sign of having heard anything. Mr. Lenoir listened a little while, saying nothing. Then he turned to a drawing-book, belonging to Julian, and began to look at the sketches there.

The children felt somehow that he was doing it for the sake of staying in the schoolroom a little longer. Into Julian's mind came the quick suspicion that somehow Mr. Lenoir must have been told of Timmy's barking and come to investigate it for himself. It was the first time he had ever come to the schoolroom!

Timmy barked again, a little more distantly. Mr. Lenoir's nose grew white at the tip. Sooty and Marybelle knew the danger-sign, and glanced at one another. That white-tipped nose usually meant a storm of temper!

'Do you hear that noise?' said Mr. Lenoir, snapping out the words.

'What noise, sir?' asked Julian, politely.

Timmy barked again.

'Don't be foolish! There's the noise again!' said Mr. Lenoir. At that moment a gull called outside the window, circling in the sea-breeze.

'Oh – that gull, sir? Yes, we often hear the gulls,' said Dick, brightly. 'Sometimes they seem to mew like a cat sir.'

'Pah!' said Mr. Lenoir, almost spitting out the word. 'I suppose you will say they also bark like a dog?'

'Well, they might, I suppose, sir,' agreed Dick, looking faintly surprised. 'After all, if they can mew like cats, there's no reason why they shouldn't bark like dogs.'

Timmy barked again very joyfully. Mr. Lenoir faced the children, in a very bad temper indeed now.

'Can't you hear that? Tell me what *that* noise is!'

The children all put their heads on one side, and pretended to listen very carefully. 'I can't hear anything,' said Dick. 'Not a thing.'

'I can hear the wind,' said Anne.

'I can hear the gulls again,' said Julian, putting his hand behind one ear.

'I can hear a door banging. Perhaps that's the noise you mean, sir!' said Sooty, with a most innocent expression. His stepfather gave him a poisonous look. He could really be very unpleasant.

'And there's a window rattling,' said Marybelle, eager to do her bit too, though she felt very frightened of her father, for she knew his sudden rages very well.

'I tell you, it's a dog, and you know it!' snapped Mr. Lenoir, the tip of his nose so white now that it looked very queer indeed. 'Where's the dog? Whose is he?'

'What dog, sir?' began Julian, frowning as if he were very puzzled indeed. 'There's no dog here that I can see.'

Mr. Lenoir glared at him, and clenched his fingers. It was quite clear that he would have liked to box Julian's ears. 'Then listen!' he hissed. 'Listen and say what you think could make that barking, if not a dog?'

They were all forced to listen, for by now they felt scared of the angry man. But fortunately Timmy made no sound at all. Either he had let the rat escape, or was now gobbling it up. Anyway, there was not a single sound from him!

'Sorry, sir but *really* I can't hear a dog barking,' said Julian, in rather an injured tone.

'Nor can I!' said Dick, and the others joined in, saying the same. Mr. Lenoir knew that this time they were speaking the truth, for he too could not hear anything.

'When I catch that dog I will have him poisoned,' he said, very slowly and clearly. 'I will not have dogs in my house.'

He turned on his heel and went out quickly, which was a very good thing, for George was quite ready to fly into one of *her* rages, and then there would have been a real battle! Anne put her hand on George's arm to stop her shouting after Mr. Lenoir.

'Don't give the game away!' she whispered. 'Don't say anything, George!'

George bit her lip. She had gone first red with rage and then white. She stamped her foot.

'How dare he, how dare he?' she burst out.

'Shut up, silly,' said Julian. 'Block will be back in a minute. We must all pretend to be awfully surprised that Mr. Lenoir thought there was a dog, because, if Block can read our lips, he mustn't know the truth.'

Block came in with the pudding at that moment, his face as blank as ever. It was the most curious face the children had ever seen, for there was never any change of expression on it at all. As Anne said, it might have been a wax mask!

'Funny how Mr. Lenoir thought there was a dog barking!' began Julian, and the others backed him up valiantly. If Block could indeed read their lips he would be puzzled to know whether there *had* been a dog barking or not!

The children escaped to Sooty's room afterwards, and held a council of war. 'What are we to do about Timmy?' said George. 'Does your stepfather know the secret way behind the walls of Smuggler's Top, Sooty? Could he possibly get in and find Timmy? Timmy might fly at him, you know.'

'Yes, he might,' said Sooty, thoughtfully. 'I don't know if Father does know about the secret passages. I mean, I expect he knows, but I don't know if he guessed where the entrances are. I found them out quite by accident.'

'I'm going home,' said George, suddenly. 'I'm not going to risk Timmy being poisoned.'

'You can't go home alone,' said Julian. 'It would look funny. If you do, we'd all have to, and then we won't have a chance to solve this mystery with Sooty.'

'No, for goodness sake don't go and leave me just now,' said Sooty, looking quite alarmed. 'It would make my father furious, simply furious.'

George hesitated. She didn't want to make trouble for Sooty, whom she liked very much. But, on the other hand, she certainly was not going to risk danger to Timmy.

'Well – I'll telephone my father and say I'm homesick and want to go back,' said George. 'I'll say I miss Mother. It's quite true, I do miss her. You others can stay on here and solve the mystery. It wouldn't be fair of you to try and keep me and Timmy here when you know I'd worry every moment in case someone got into the secret passage and put down poisoned meat for him to eat.'

The others hadn't thought of this. That would be terrible. Julian sighed. He would have to let George have her own way after all.

'All right. You telephone to your father,' he said. 'There's a phone downstairs. Do it now if you like. There won't be anyone about now, I don't suppose.'

George slipped down the passage, out of the door there, and down the stairs to where the telephone was enclosed in a dark little cupboard. She asked for the number she wanted.

There was a long wait. Then she heard the buzzing noise – brr – brr – brr – brr – that told her that the telephone bell at Kirrin Cottage was ringing. She began to plan what she should say to her father. She must, she really must go home with Timmy. She didn't know how she was going to explain about Timmy – perhaps she needn't explain at all. But she meant to go home that day or the next!

'Brr – brr – brr – brr' said the bell at the other end. It went on and on, and nobody answered it. She did not hear her father's familiar voice – only the bell that went on ringing. Why did nobody answer?

The operator at the exchange spoke to her. 'I'm sorry There's no reply.'

George put down the receiver miserably. Perhaps her parents were out? She would have to try again later on.

Poor George tried three times, but each time there was the same result. No reply. As she was coming out of the telephone cupboard for the third time, Mrs. Lenoir saw her.

'Have you been trying to telephone to your home?' she said. 'Haven't you heard any news?'

'I haven't had a letter yet,' said George. 'I've tried three times to telephone Kirrin Cottage but each time there is no reply.'

'Well, we heard this morning that it is impossible to live in Kirrin Cottage while the men are hammering and knocking everywhere,' said Mrs. Lenoir, in her gentle voice. 'We heard from your mother. She said that the noise was driving your father mad, and they were going away for a week or so, till things were better. But Mr. Lenoir at once wrote and asked them here. We shall know tomorrow, because we have asked them to telephone a reply. We could not get them on the telephone today, of course, any more than you could, because they have gone away already.'

'Oh,' said George, surprised at all this news and wondering why her mother had not written to tell her too.

'Your mother said she had written to you,' said Mrs. Lenoir. 'Maybe the letter will come by the next post. The posts are often most peculiar here. It will be a pleasure to have your parents if they can come. Mr. Lenoir particularly wants to meet your clever father. He thinks he is quite a genius.'

George said no more but went back to the others, her face serious. She opened Sooty's door, and the others saw at once that she had had news of some sort.

'I can't go home with Timothy,' said George. 'Mother and Father can't stand the noise the workmen make, and they have both gone away!'

'Bad luck!' said Sooty. 'All the same, I'm glad you'll have to stay here, George. I should hate to lose you or Timmy.'

'Your mother has written to ask my mother and father to come and stay here too,' said George. 'What I shall do about Timmy I don't know! And they are sure to ask questions about him too. I can't tell a downright lie and say I left him with Alf the fisher-boy, or anything like that. I can't think *what* to do!'

'We'll think of something,' promised Sooty. 'Perhaps I can get one of the villagers to look after him for us. That would be a very good idea.'

'Oh yes!' said George, cheering up. 'Why didn't I think of that before? Let's ask someone quickly, Sooty.'

But it was impossible to do anything that day because Mrs. Lenoir asked them to go down into the drawing-room after tea, and have a game with her. So none of them could go out to find someone to look after Timmy.

'Never mind,' thought George. 'He'll be safe tonight on my bed! Tomorrow will be soon enough.'

It was the first time that Mrs. Lenoir had asked them down to be with her. 'You see, Mr. Lenoir is out tonight on important business,' she explained. 'He has had to go to the mainland with the car. He doesn't like his evenings disturbed when he is at home, so I haven't been able to see as much of you all as I should have liked. But tonight I can.'

Julian wondered if Mr. Lenoir had gone to the mainland on smuggling business! Somehow the smuggled goods must be taken across to the mainland – and if all that signalling business the other night had to do with Mr. Lenoir's smuggling then maybe he had now gone to dispose of the goods!

The telephone bell rang shrilly. Mrs Lenoir got up. 'I expect that is your mother or father on the phone,' she said to George. 'Maybe I shall have news for you! Perhaps your parents will be arriving here tomorrow.'

She went out into the hall. The children waited anxiously. Would George's parents come or not?

Chapter Twelve

BLOCK GETS A SURPRISE

Mrs. Lenoir came back after a time. She smiled at George.

'That was your father,' she said. 'He is coming to-morrow, but not your mother. They went to your aunt's, and your mother says she thinks she must stay and help her, because your aunt is not very well. But your father would like to come, because he wants to discuss his latest experiments with Mr. Lenoir, who is very interested in them. It will be very nice to have him.'

The children would very much rather have had Aunt Fanny instead of Uncle Quentin, who could be very difficult at times. But still, he would probably be talking with Mr. Lenoir most of the time, so that would be all right!

They finished their game with Mrs. Lenoir and went up to bed. George was to get Timmy to take him to her room. Sooty went to see that the coast was clear. He could not see Block anywhere. His stepfather was still away from the house. Sarah was singing in the kitchen and the little kitchen-maid, Harriet, was knitting there in a corner.

'Block must be out,' thought Sooty, and went to tell George that the coast was clear. As he went across the landing to the long passage that led to his own room, the boy noticed two black lumps sticking out at the bottom of the thick curtains drawn across the landing window. He looked at them in surprise, and then recognized them. He grinned.

'So old Block suspects we have a dog, and he thinks

it sleeps in George's room or Julian's, and he's posted himself there to watch!' he thought 'Aha! I'll give friend Block a nasty shock!'

He ran to tell the others. George listened, alarmed. But Sooty, as usual, had a plan.

'We'll give Block an awful shock!' he said. 'I'll get a rope, and we'll all go down to the landing. I'll suddenly yell out that there's a robber hiding behind the curtains and I'll pounce on Block, and give him a few good punches. Then, with your help, Julian and Dick, I'll fold him up well in the curtains – a good jerk will bring them down on top of him as well!'

The others began to laugh. It would be fun to play a trick on Block. He really was such an unpleasant fellow. A good lesson would do him no harm.

'While all the excitement is beginning I'll slip by with Timmy,' said George. 'I only hope he won't want to join in! He might give Block a good nip!'

'Well, hold on to Timmy firmly,' said Julian. 'Get him into your room quickly. Now – are we ready?'

They were. Feeling excited they crept down the long passage that led to the door which opened out on to the landing where Block was hiding. They saw the curtains move very slightly as they came along. Block was watching.

George waited with Timmy at the passage door, not showing herself at all Then, with a yell from Sooty, a really blood-curdling yell that made both George and Timmy jump, things began to happen!

Sooty flung himself on the hidden Block with all his might. 'A robber! Help, a robber hiding here!' he shouted.

Block jumped, and began to struggle. Sooty got in two or three well-aimed punches. Block had often got him into trouble with his father, and now Sooty was getting a bit of his own back! Julian and Dick rushed to help.

A violent tug at the curtains brought them down on Block's head! Not only that, the curtain pole descended on him too, and knocked him sideways. Poor Block – he was completely taken by surprise, and could do nothing against the three determined boys. Even Anne gave a hand, though Marybelle stood apart, enjoying the fun though not daring to take part in it.

Just as it all began George slipped by with Timmy. But Timmy could not bear to miss the fun. He dragged behind George, and would not go with her.

She tried to force him, her hand on his collar. But Timmy had seen a nice fat leg waving about near him, protruding from the curtain. He pounced on it.

There was an agonized yell from Block. Certainly Timmy could nip hard with his sharp white teeth. He worried at the kicking leg for a few seconds, and then had a sharp slap from George. Shocked, Timmy let go the leg and humbly followed his mistress. She never slapped him! She must indeed be angry with him. With tail well down Timmy followed her into the bedroom and got under the bed at once. He poked his head out and looked beseechingly at George with big brown eyes.

'Oh, Timmy – I *had* to slap you!' said George, and she knelt down by the big dog and patted his head. 'You see, you might have spoilt everything if you'd been seen. As it is I'm sure you bit Block and I don't know how we're going to explain that! Lie quietly now, old fellow. I'm going out to join the others.'

Timmy's tail thumped softly on the floor. George ran out of the room and joined the others on the landing. They were having a fine game with Block, who was yelling and wriggling and struggling for all he was worth.

He was wrapped up in the blanket like a caterpillar inside a cocoon. His head was completely covered and he could see nothing.

Suddenly Mr. Lenoir appeared in the hall below, with a very scared Mrs. Lenoir beside him. 'What's all this?' thundered Sooty's stepfather. 'Have you gone mad? How dare you behave like this at this time of night?'

'Sir, we've caught a robber and tied him up,' panted Sooty.

Mr. Lenoir ran up the stairs two steps at a time, amazed. He saw the kicking figure on the ground well-tied up in the heavy curtains. 'A robber! Do you mean a burglar? Where did you find him?'

'He was hiding behind the curtains, sir!' said Julian. 'We managed to get hold of him and tie him up before he could escape. Could you call the police sir?'

An anguished voice came from inside of the curtains. 'Let me go! I've been bitten! Let me go!'

'Good heavens! You've got Block tied up there!' said Mr. Lenoir, in amazement and anger. 'Untie him, quickly.'

'But, sir – it can't be Block. He was hiding behind those curtains at the window,' protested Sooty.

'Do as you're told,' commanded Mr. Lenoir, getting angry. Anne looked at the tip of his nose. Yes, it was turning white, as usual!

The boys reluctantly undid the ropes. Block angrily parted the curtains that enfolded him, and looked out, his usually blank face crimson with rage and fright.

'I won't stand this sort of thing!' he raged. 'Look here, at my leg, sir! I've been bitten. Only a dog could have done that. See my leg?'

Sure enough there were the marks of teeth on his leg,

slowly turning purple. Timmy had taken a good nip, and almost gone through the skin.

'There's no dog here,' said Mrs. Lenoir, coming timidly up the stairs at last. 'You couldn't have been bitten by a dog, Block.'

'Who bit him, then?' demanded Mr. Lenoir, turning fiercely on poor Mrs. Lenoir.

'Do you think *I* could have bitten him, sir, in my excitement?' suddenly said Sooty, to the enormous surprise of the others, and to their immense amusement. He spoke very seriously with a worried look on his face. 'When I lose my temper, sir, I hardly know what I do. Do you think I bit him?'

'Pah!' said Mr. Lenoir, in disgust. 'Don't talk nonsense, boy! I'll have you whipped if I think you go about biting people. Get up, Block. You're not badly hurt.'

'My teeth do feel a bit funny, now I come to think of it,' said Sooty, opening and shutting his mouth as if to see if they were all right. I think I'd better go and clean them, sir. I feel as if I've got the taste of Block's ankle in my mouth. And it isn't nice.'

Mr. Lenoir, driven to fury by Sooty's impudence, reached out swiftly to box the boy's ears. But Sooty dodged and ran back up the passage. 'Just going to clean my teeth!' he called, and the others tried to keep from laughing. The idea of Sooty biting anyone was absurd. It was quite obvious, however, that neither Mr. nor Mrs. Lenoir guessed what had bitten Block.

'Go to bed, all of you,' ordered Mr. Lenoir. 'I hope I shall not have to complain of you to your father tomorrow when he comes – or your uncle, as it may be. I don't know which of you are his children, and which not. I'm surprised at you making such a nuisance of yourselves in somebody else's house. Tying up my servant! If he leaves, it will be your fault!'

The children hoped fervently that Block *would* leave. It would be marvellous to have the deaf, blank-faced fellow out of the house. He was on the watch for Timmy, they felt sure. He would snoop about till he got Timmy or one of them into trouble.

But Block was still there next morning. He came into the schoolroom with the breakfast, his face almost as blank as usual. He gave Sooty an evil look.

'You look out for yourself,' he said, in a curiously soft voice. 'You look out. Something's going to happen to you one of these days. Yes – and that dog too! I know you've got a dog, see? You can't deceive *me*.'

The children said nothing, but looked at one another. Sooty grinned, and rapped out a gay little tattoo on the table with his spoon.

'Dark, dire, dreadful threats!' he said. 'You look out for yourself too, Block. Any more snooping about, and you'll find yourself tied up again – yes, and I might bite you again too. You never know. My teeth feel quite ready for it this morning.'

He bared his teeth at Block, who made no reply at all, but merely looked as if he had not heard a word. The man went out, and closed the door softly behind him.

'Nasty bit of work, isn't he?' said Sooty. But George felt rather alarmed. She feared Block. There was something cold and clever and bad about those narrow eyes of his. She longed with all her heart to get Timmy out of the house.

She got a terrible shock that morning! Sooty came to her, looking agitated. 'I say! What do you think? Your father's going to have *my* room. I've got to sleep with Julian and Dick. Block is taking all my things from my

room to theirs this very minute, with Sarah. I hope we shall have a chance to get him out all right, before your father comes!'

'Oh Sooty!' said George, in despair. 'I'll go and see if I can get him at once.'

She went off, pretending to go to Marybelle's room for something. But Block was still in Sooty's room. And there he stayed, cleaning it all morning!

George was very worried about Timmy. He would wonder why she hadn't fetched him. He would miss his walk. She hovered about the passage all morning, getting into Sarah's way as she carried clothes from Sooty's old room to Julian's.

Block gave George some curious looks. He walked with a limp to show that his leg was bad from the bite. He left the room at last and George darted in. But Block returned almost at once and she dashed back into Marybelle's room. Again Block left and went down the passage, and again the desperate little girl rushed into Sooty's room.

But Block was back before she could even open the cupboard door. 'What are you doing in this room?' he said, roughly. 'I haven't cleaned it all morning to have children in here messing it up again! Clear out of it!'

George went – and then once more waited for Block to go. He would have to see to the luncheon soon! He went at last. George rushed to the door of Sooty's room, eager to get poor Timmy.

But she couldn't open the door. It was locked – and Block had taken the key!

POOR GEORGE!

By now George was in despair. She felt as if she was in a nightmare. She went to find Sooty. He was in Julian's room, next to hers, washing his hands ready for lunch.

'Sooty! I shall have to get into the secret passage the way you first took us in,' she said. 'Through that little study-room of your father's – you know, where the sliding panels are.'

'We can't,' said Sooty, looking rather alarmed. 'He uses it now, and he'd half-kill anyone who went in there. He's got the records of all his experiments there, and he's put them ready to show your father.'

'I don't care,' said George, desperately. 'I've got to get in there somehow. Timmy may starve!'

'Not Timmy! He'll live on the rats in the passages!' said Sooty. 'Timmy could always look after himself, I bet!'

'Well, he'd die of thirst then,' said George, obstinately. 'There's no water in those secret passages. You know that!'

George could hardly eat any lunch because she was so worried. She made up her mind somehow to get into that little study-room, and see if she could open the entrance into the wall behind the panels. Then she would slip in and get Timmy. She didn't care what happened; she was going to get Timmy.

'I shan't tell the others, though,' she thought. 'They would only try and stop me, or offer to do it themselves, and I don't trust anyone but myself to do this. Timmy's my dog, and *I'm* going to save him!'

After lunch, everyone went to Julian's room to discuss things. George went with them. But after a few minutes she left them. 'Back in a minute,' she said. They took no notice and went on discussing how to rescue Timmy. It really did seem as if the only way was to raid the study, and try and get into the secret passage without being seen.

'But my stepfather works there now,' said Sooty. 'And I shouldn't be surprised if he locks the door when he leaves the room.'

George didn't come back. After about ten minutes Anne grew puzzled.

'What can George be doing? It must be about ten minutes since she went.'

'Oh, she's probably gone to see if my old room is unlocked yet,' said Sooty, getting up. 'I'll peep out and see if she's about.'

She wasn't. She didn't seem to be anywhere! She wasn't in the passage that led to Sooty's old room; she couldn't be in that room because it was still locked, and she wasn't in Marybelle's room.

Sooty peeped in George's own room, the one she shared with Anne. But that was empty too. He went downstairs and snooped around a bit. No George!

He went back to the others, puzzled.

'I can't find her anywhere,' he said. 'Where can she be?'

Anne looked alarmed. This was such a queer house, with queer happenings. She wished George would come.

'She's not gone into that little study-room, has she?' said Julian, suddenly. It would be just like George to try and get into the lion's den!

'I didn't think of that,' said Sooty. 'Silly of me. I'll go and see.'

He went down the stairs. He made his way cautiously to his father's study. He stood quietly outside the shut door. There was no sound from inside. Was his father there or not?

Sooty debated whether to open the door and peep in or whether to knock. He decided to knock. Then, if his father answered he could rush back upstairs before the door could be opened, and his father would not know whom to scold for the interruption.

So he knocked, very smartly, Rap-rap.

'Who's that?' came his stepfather's irritable voice. 'Come in! Am I to have no peace?'

Sooty fled upstairs at once. He went to the others. 'George can't be in the study,' he said. 'My stepfather's there, and he didn't sound in too good a temper either.'

'Then *where* can she be?' said Julian, looking worried. 'I do wish she wouldn't go off without telling us where she's going. She must be somewhere about. She wouldn't go very far from Timmy.'

They all had a good hunt over the house, even going into the kitchen. Block was there, reading a paper. 'What do you want?' he said. 'You won't get it, whatever it is.'

'We don't want anything from *you*,' said Sooty. 'How's your poor bad bitten leg?'

Block looked so unpleasantly at them that they all retreated from the kitchen in a hurry. Sooty put Julian and Dick on guard, and went up to the staff bedrooms to see if by any chance George had gone there. A silly idea, he knew, but George must be somewhere!

She wasn't there, of course. The children went back gloomily to Julian's room. 'This beastly house!' said Julian. 'I can't say I like it. Sorry to say so, Sooty, but it's a queer place with a queer feeling about it.'

Sooty was not hurt at all. 'Oh, I agree with you,' he

said. 'I've always thought the same myself. So has Mother, and so has Marybelle. It's my stepfather that likes it.'

'Where *is* George?' said Anne. 'I keep on and on trying to think. There's only one place I'm certain she's not in — and that's your stepfather's study, Sooty. Even George wouldn't dare to go there while your stepfather was there.'

But Anne was wrong. The study was the very place where George was at that very moment!

The little girl had made up her mind that it was best to try and get in there, and wait for a chance to open the sliding panel. So she had slipped downstairs, gone across the hall, and tried the door of the study. It was locked.

'Blow!' said George, desperately. 'Everything is against me and Timmy. How can I get in? I must, I must!'

She slipped out of the side-door near the study and went into the little yard on to which the study-window looked. Could she get in there?

But the window was barred! So that was no good either. She went back again, wishing she could find the key to unlock the door. But it was nowhere to be seen.

Suddenly she heard Mr. Lenoir's voice in the room across the hall. In a panic George lifted up the lid of a big wooden chest nearby, and climbed hurriedly into it. She closed the lid over her, and knelt there, waiting, heart beating fast.

Mr. Lenoir came across the hall. He was going to his study. 'I shall get everything ready to show my visitor when he comes,' he called to his wife. 'Don't disturb me at all. I shall be very busy indeed.'

George heard the sound of a key being put into the study door. It turned. The door opened and shut with a click.

But it was not locked again from the inside. George knelt in the dark chest and considered matters. She meant to get into that study. She meant to get through the entrance into the secret passage, where Tim was. That passage led from the study to Sooty's old bedroom, and somewhere in that passage was Timmy.

What she was going to do once she had Timmy she didn't quite know. Perhaps Sooty would take him to someone who could look after him for her, someone on Castaway Hill.

She heard the sound of Mr. Lenoir coughing. She heard the shuffling of papers. Then she heard the click of a cupboard being opened and shut. Mr. Lenoir was evidently busy!

Then he gave an exclamation of annoyance. He said something in an irritable voice that sounded like 'Now where did I put that?'

Then the door opened very suddenly and Mr. Lenoir came out. George had just time to close down the lid, which she had opened to let in fresh air. She knelt in the chest, trembling, as Mr. Lenoir passed there and went on across the hall.

George suddenly knew that this was her chance. Mr. Lenoir might be gone for a few minutes and give her time to open that panel in the wall! She lifted the lid of the chest, and jumped out quickly. She ran into the study, and went to the place where Sooty had pressed the panelling.

But before she could even run her fingers over the smooth brown oak, she heard returning footsteps! Mr. Lenoir had hardly been half a minute. He was coming back at once.

In a panic poor George looked round for somewhere to hide. There was a large sofa against one wall. George crawled behind it, finding just room to crouch there without being seen. She was hardly there before Mr. Lenoir entered the room, shut the door, and sat down at his desk. He switched on a big lamp over it, and bent to look at some documents.

George hardly dared to breathe. Her heart bumped against her ribs and seemed to make a terrible noise. It was very uncomfortable behind the sofa, but she did not dare to move.

She could not think what in the world to do. It would be terrible to be there for hours! What would the others think? They would soon be looking for her.

They were. Even at that moment Sooty was outside the study door, pondering whether to go in or to knock. He knocked smartly – rap-rap – and George almost jumped out of her skin!

She heard Mr. Lenoir's impatient voice. 'Who's that? Come in! Am I to have no peace?'

There was no answer. No one came in. Mr. Lenoir called again. 'Come in, I say!'

Still no answer. He strode to the door and flung it open angrily. No one was there. Sooty had fled upstairs at once.

'Those tiresome children, I suppose,' muttered Mr. Lenoir. 'Well, if any of them comes and knocks again and goes away, I'll punish them properly. Bed and bread and water for them!'

He sounded fierce. George wished she was anywhere but in his study. What would he say if he knew she was only three or four feet away from him?

Mr. Lenoir worked for about half an hour, and poor George got stiffer and stiffer, and more and more uncomfortable. Then she heard Mr. Lenoir yawn, and her heart felt lighter. Perhaps he would have a nap! That would be good luck. She might creep out then, and try to get into the secret passage.

Mr. Lenoir yawned again. Then he pushed his papers aside and went to the sofa. He lay down on it and pulled the rug there over his knees. He settled himself down as if for a good sleep.

The sofa creaked under him. George tried to hold her breath again, afraid that now he was so near to her he would certainly hear her.

Soon a small snore came to her ears. Then another and another. Mr. Lenoir was asleep! George waited for a few minutes. The snores went on, a little louder. Surely it would be safe now to creep from her hiding-place?

George began to move, very cautiously and quietly. She crept to the end of the sofa. She squeezed out from behind it. Still the snores went on.

She stood upright and went on tiptoe to the panel that had slid aside. She began to press here and there with her fingers, trying to find the spot that would move the panel to one side.

She couldn't seem to find it. She grew red with anxiety. She cast a glance at the sleeping Mr. Lenoir, and worked feverishly at the panel. Where was the spot to press, oh, where was it?

Then a stern voice came from behind her, making her jump almost out of her skin.

'And what exactly do you think you are doing, my boy? How dare you come into my study and mess about like this?'

George turned round and faced Mr. Lenoir. He always thought she was a boy! She didn't know what to say. He looked very angry indeed, and the tip of his nose was already white.

George was frightened. She ran to the door, but Mr.

Lenoir caught her before she opened it. He shook her hard.

'What were you doing in my study? Was it you who knocked and ran away? Do you think it is funny to play tricks like that? I'll soon teach you that it isn't?'

He opened the door and called loudly. 'Block! Come here! Sarah, tell Block I want him.'

Block appeared from the kitchen, his face as blank as usual. Mr. Lenoir wrote something down quickly on a piece of paper and gave it him to read. Block nodded.

'I've told him to take you to your room, lock you in, and give you nothing but bread and water for the rest of the day,' said Mr. Lenoir, fiercely. 'That will teach you to behave yourself in the future. Any more nonsense, and I'll whip you myself.'

'My father won't be very pleased when he hears you're punishing me like this,' began George in a trembling voice. But Mr. Lenoir sneered.

'Pah! Wait till he hears from me how you have mis-behaved yourself, and I am sure he will agree with me. Now go, and you will not be allowed out of your room till tomorrow. I will make your excuses to your father, when he comes.'

Poor George was propelled upstairs by Block, who was only too delighted to be punishing one of the children. As she came to the door of the room George shouted to the others who were in Julian's room next door.

'Julian! Dick! Help me! Quick, help me!'

Chapter Fourteen

A VERY PUZZLING THING

JULIAN, Dick, and the others rushed out at once, just in time to see Block shove George roughly into her room and shut the door. There was a click as he locked it.

'Here! What are you doing?' cried Julian, indignantly.

Block took no notice, but turned to go. Julian caught hold of his arm, and yelled loudly in his ear. 'Unlock that door at once! Do you hear?'

Block gave no sign whether he had or not. He shook off Julian's hand, but the boy put it back again at once, getting angry.

'Mr. Lenoir gave me orders to punish that girl,' said Block, looking at Julian out of his cold, narrow eyes.

'Well, you jolly well unlock that door,' commanded Julian, and he tried to snatch the key from Block. With sudden vicious strength the man lifted his hand and struck Julian, sending him half across the landing. Then he went swiftly downstairs to the kitchen.

Julian looked after him, a little scared. 'The brute!' he said. 'He's as strong as a horse. George, George, whatever's happened?'

George answered angrily from the locked bedroom. She told the others everything, and they listened in silence. 'Bad luck, George,' said Dick. 'Poor old girl! Just as you were feeling for the opening to the passage too!'

'I must apologize for my stepfather,' said Sooty. 'He has such a terrible temper. He wouldn't have punished you like this if he had thought you were a girl. But he keeps thinking you're a boy.'

'I don't care,' said George. 'I don't care about any punishment. It's only that I'm so worried about Timmy. Well, I suppose I'll have to stay here now, till I'm let out tomorrow. I shan't eat anything that Block brings me, you can tell him. I don't want to see his horrid face again!'

'How shall I go to bed tonight?' wailed Anne. 'All my things are in your room, George.'

'You'll have to sleep with me,' said little Marybelle, who looked very frightened. 'I can lend you a nightie. Oh dear – what will George's father say when he comes? I hope he will say that George is to be set free at once.'

'Well, he won't,' said George, from behind the locked door. 'He'll just think I've been in one of my bad moods, and he won't mind my being punished at all. Oh dear – I wish Mother was coming too.'

The others were very upset about George, as well as

about Timmy. Things seemed to be going very wrong
indeed. At tea-time they went to the schoolroom to have
tea, wishing they could take George some of the choco-
late cake set ready for them.

George felt lonely when the others had gone to tea.
It was five o'clock. She was hungry. She wanted Timmy.
She was angry and miserable, and longed to escape.
She went to the window and looked out.

Her room looked straight down the cliff-side, just as
Sooty's old room did. Below was the city-wall that ran
round the town, going unevenly up and down as it followed the contours of the hillside.

George knew that she could not jump down to the
wall. She might roll off it and fall straight down to the
marsh below. That would be horrible. Then she suddenly
remembered the rope-ladder that they used when they
got down into the pit each day.

It had at first been kept in Marybelle's room, on the
shelf in the cupboard, but since the children had been
scared by knowing that someone had tried the handle
of the door one morning, they had decided to keep the
ladder in George's room for safety. They were afraid
that perhaps Block might go snooping round Marybelle's
room and find it. So George had smuggled it to her
own room, and hidden it in her suitcase, which she had
locked.

Now, her hands shaking a little with excitement, she
unlocked her suitcase and took out the rope-ladder. She
might perhaps escape out of the window with it. She
looked out again, the rope in her hands.

But windows overlooked the city-wall just there. The
kitchen too must be just below, and maybe Block would
see her climbing down. That would never do. She must
wait till it was twilight.

When the others came back she told them what she was going to do, speaking in a low voice through the door.

'I'll get down on the wall, walk along it for some way, and then jump down and creep back, she said. 'You get some food for me somehow, and I'll have it. Then tonight, when everyone has gone to bed I'll get into the study again and find the way through to the secret passage. Sooty can help me. Then I can get Timmy.'

'Right,' said Sooty. 'Wait till it's fairly dark before you go down the ladder, though. Block has gone to his room with a bad headache, but Sarah and Harriet are in the kitchen, and you don't want to be seen.'

So, when the twilight hung like a soft purple curtain over the house, George slid down the rope-ladder out of the window. She only needed to let about a quarter of it out for it was far too long for such a short distance.

She fastened it to the legs of her heavy little oak bed. Then she climbed out of the window and slid quietly down the rope-ladder.

She passed the kitchen window, which fortunately had its blinds drawn down now. She landed squarely on the old wall. She had brought a torch with her so that she could see.

She debated with herself what to do. She did not want to run any risk of coming up against either Block or Mr. Lenoir. Perhaps it would be best to walk along the wall till she came to some part of the town she knew. Then she could jump off and make her way cautiously back up the hill, looking out for the others.

So she began to walk along the broad top of the old wall. It was very rough and uneven in places, and many stones were missing. But her torch showed a steady light and she did not miss her footing.

The wall ran round some stables, then round the backs of some quaint old shops. Then it ran round a big yard belonging to some house, and then round the house itself. Then down it went, around some more houses.

George could look into those windows that were not curtained. Lights shone out from them now. It was queer being able to see into the windows without being seen. A little family sat at a meal in one room, their faces cheerful and happy. An old man sat alone in another, reading and smoking.

A woman sat listening to a wireless, knitting, as George silently walked on the wall outside her window. Nobody heard her. Nobody saw her.

Then she came to another house, a big one. The wall ran close against it, for it was built where the cliff ran steeply down to the marsh just there.

There was a lighted window there. George glanced in as she passed. Then she stood still in great surprise.

Surely, surely that was Block in there! He had his back to her, but she could have sworn it was Block. The same head, the same ears, the same shoulders!

Who was he talking to? George tried to see – and all at once she knew. He was talking to Mr. Barling, whom everyone said was a smuggler – *the* smuggler of Castaway Hill!

But wait a minute – could it be Block? Block was deaf, and this man evidently wasn't. He was listening to Mr. Barling, that was plain, and was answering him, though George could not hear the words, of course.

'I oughtn't to be snooping like this,' said George to herself. 'But it's very strange, very puzzling and very interesting. If only the man would turn round I'd know at once if it was Block!'

But he didn't turn. He just sat in his chair, his back to George. Mr. Barling, his long face lighted up by the nearby lamp, was talking animatedly, and Block, if it *was* Block, was listening intently and nodding his head in agreement every now and again.

George felt puzzled, If she only knew for certain that it was Block! But why should he be talking to Mr. Barling – and wasn't he stone deaf after all then?

George jumped down from the wall into a dark little passage and made her way through the town, up to Smuggler's Top. Outside the front door, hiding in the shadows was Sooty. He laid his hand on George's arm, making her jump.

'Come on in. I've left the side-door open. We've got a fine spread for you!'

The two slipped in at the side-door, tiptoed past the study, across the hall, and up to Julian's bedroom. Truly there was a spread there!

'I went and raided the larder,' said Sooty, with satisfaction. 'Harriet was out, and Sarah had run along to the post. Block has gone to bed for a rest, because, he said, he had such an awful headache.'

'Oh,' said George, 'then it couldn't have been Block I saw. And yet I'm as certain as certain can be that it was!'

'Whatever do you mean?' asked the others, in surprise. George sat down on the floor and began to gobble up cakes and tarts, for she was terribly hungry. Between her mouthfuls she told them how she had got out of the window, walked along the city-wall, and found herself unexpectedly by Mr. Barling's house.

'And I looked into a lighted window there, and saw Block talking to Mr. Barling – and listening to him and answering him!' she said.

The others could not believe this. 'Did you see his face?' asked Julian.

'No,' said George. 'But I'm *certain* it was Block. Go and peep into his room and see if he's there, Sooty. He wouldn't be back yet from Mr. Barling's, because he had a glass full of something or other, which would take him some time to drink. Go and peep.'

Sooty vanished. He came back quickly. 'He's in bed!' he said. 'I could see the shape of his body and the dark patch of his head. Are there *two* Blocks then? Whatever does this mean?'

Chapter Fifteen

STRANGE HAPPENINGS

IT certainly was very puzzling – most of all to George, who felt so certain it had been Block talking to the well-known smuggler. The others did not feel so certain, especially as George admitted that she had not seen his face.

'Is my father here yet?' asked George, suddenly, remembering that he was supposed to come that evening.

'Yes. Just arrived,' said Sooty. 'Just before you came. I nearly got run over by the car! Just hopped aside in time. I was out there waiting for you.'

'What are our plans?' asked George. 'I'll have to get Timmy tonight, or he'll be frantic. I think I'd better go and climb back through my window again now, in case Block comes along and finds I've disappeared. I'll wait till everyone is in bed and then I'll slip out of the window again, and you must let me into the house, Sooty, please. Then I'll go to the study with you and you must open the secret way for me. Then I'll find Timmy and everything will be all right.'

'I don't see that everything will be all right,' said Sooty, doubtfully. 'But anyway, your plan is the only one to follow. You'd better get back into your room now, if you've had enough to eat.'

'I'll take a few buns back with me,' said George, stuffing them into her pocket. 'Sooty, come and knock at my door when everyone is in bed and I'll know then that it's safe for me to slip out of the window, and come into the house again.'

It wasn't long before George was back in her room once

more – just in time too, for Block appeared a little while after with a plate of dry bread and a glass of water. He unlocked the door and put them on the table.

'Your supper,' he said. George looked at his blank face and disliked it so much that she felt she must do something about it. So she took up the water and threw it deftly at the back of his head. It dripped down his neck and made him jump. Block took a step towards her, his eyes gleaming – but Julian and Dick were by the door, and he did not dare to strike her.

'I'll pay you out for that,' he said. 'See? You will never get that dog of yours back again!'

He went out and locked the door. Julian called through as soon as he had gone.

'What did you do that for, you idiot? He's a bad enemy to make.'

'I know. I just couldn't help it somehow,' said George, forlornly. 'I wish I hadn't now.'

The others had to go down to see Mr. Lenoir. They left George feeling lonely. It was horrid to be locked up like this, even though she could escape through the window whenever she wanted to. She listened for the others to come back.

They soon did, and reported their meeting with George's father.

'Uncle Quentin is awfully tired and a bit cross, and frightfully annoyed with you for misbehaving,' said Julian, through the door. 'He said you were to be locked up the whole of tomorrow too, if you don't apologize.'

George didn't mean to apologize. She couldn't bear Mr. Lenoir, with his false smiles and laughter, and his sudden queer rages. She said nothing.

'We've got to go and have our supper now,' said Sooty. 'We'll save you some of it as soon as Block goes out of the room. Look out for a knocking on your door tonight. It'll be me, telling you everyone's in bed.'

George lay on her bed, thinking. Many things puzzled her. She couldn't get them straight somehow. The signaller in the tower – the queer man, Block – Mr. Barling's talk to a man who looked so like Block; but Block was all the time in his bed at home. As she lay thinking, her eyes closed, and she fell asleep.

Anne went to bed with Marybelle, and came to whisper good-night to her. The boys all went into the next room, for Sooty was now to share Julian's and Dick's bedroom. George woke up enough to say good-night and then slept again.

At midnight she awoke with a jump. Someone was

knocking softly and impatiently on her door. It was Sooty.

'Coming!' whispered George through the door, and took up her torch. She went to the window and was soon safely down the rope-ladder. She jumped down from the wall, and went to the side-door of the house. Sooty was there. She slipped in thankfully.

'Everyone's gone to bed,' whispered Sooty. 'I thought your father and my stepfather were never going. They stayed talking in the study for ages!'

'Come on. Let's go there,' said George, impatiently. They went to the study-door, and Sooty turned the handle.

It was locked again! He pushed hard, but it wasn't a bit of good. It was well and truly locked!

'We might have thought of that,' said George, in despair. 'Blow, blow, blow! What are we to do now?'

Sooty thought for a few moments. Then he spoke in a low voice, in George's ear.

'There's only one thing left to do, George. I must creep into your father's room – my old bedroom – when he is asleep – and I must get into the cupboard there, open the entrance to the secret passage, and slip in that way. I'll find Timmy and bring him back the same way, hoping that your father won't wake!'

'Oh! Would you really do that for me?' said George, gratefully. 'You *are* a good friend, Sooty! Would you rather I did it?'

'No. I know the way up and down that passage better than you do,' said Sooty. 'It's a bit frightening to be all alone there at midnight too. I'll go.'

George went with Sooty up the stairs, across the wide landing, to the door at the end of the passage that led to Sooty's old room, where George's father was now sleeping. When they got there, George pulled his arm.

'Sooty! the buzzer will go as soon as you open the door – and it will wake my father and warn him.'

'Idiot! I disconnected it as soon as I knew my room was to be changed,' said Sooty, scornfully. 'As if I wouldn't think of that!'

He opened the door that led into the passage. He crept up to his old room. The door was shut. He and George listened intently.

'Your father sounds a bit restless,' said Sooty. 'I'll wait my chance to creep in, George, and then, as soon as possible, I'll slip into the cupboard and open the secret passage to find Tim. As soon as I've got Timmy I'll bring him along to you. You could wait in Marybelle's room if you liked. Anne's there too.'

George crept into the room next door, where Anne and Marybelle lay fast asleep. She left the door open, so that she might hear when Sooty returned. How lovely it would be to have dear old Timmy again! He would lick her and lick her.

Sooty crept into the room where George's father lay, half-asleep. He made no sound. He knew every creaking board and avoided them. He made his way quietly to a big chair, meaning to hide behind it till he was certain George's father was sound asleep.

For some time the man in the bed tossed and turned. He was tired with his long journey, and his mind was excited with his talk with Mr. Lenoir. He muttered now and again, and Sooty began to feel he would never be sound asleep! He grew sleepy himself, and yawned silently.

At last George's father grew quiet and peaceful. No more creaks came from the bed. Sooty cautiously moved out from behind the chair.

Then suddenly something startled him. He heard a

sound over by the window! But what could it be? It was a very small sound, like a tiny creak of a door.

The night was rather dark, but the window, its curtains pulled right back, could easily be seen as a square of grey. Sooty fixed his eyes on it. Was someone opening the window?

No. The window did not move. But something queer was happening under it, near the sill.

A big window-seat was built in under the window, wide and comfortable. Sooty knew it well! He had sat on it hundreds of times to look out of the window. Now, what was happening to it?

It looked as if the top, or lid of the seat was slowly moving upwards, bit by bit. Sooty was puzzled. He had never known it could be opened like that. It had always been screwed down, and he had thought it was just a seat and nothing else. But now it looked as if someone had unscrewed the top, and had hidden himself inside, lifting up the top like a lid when he thought it was safe.

Sooty stared at the upward-moving lid, quite fascinated. Who was in there? Why had he hidden? It was rather frightening, seeing the lid move slowly, bit by bit.

At last the lid was wide open and rested against the window-pane. A big figure cautiously and slowly got out, not making the slightest sound. Sooty felt his hair rising up on his head. He was afraid, terribly afraid. He could not utter a sound.

The figure tiptoed over to the bed. He made a quick and sudden movement, and there was a stifled sound from George's father. Sooty guessed he had been gagged, so that he could not cry out. Still the boy could not move or speak. He had never been so scared in all his life.

The intruder lifted the limp body from the bed, and went to the window-seat. He put George's father into the darkness there. What he had done to make him unable to struggle Sooty didn't know. He only knew that poor George's father was being put down in the window-seat, and couldn't seem to move a hand to help himself!

The boy suddenly found his voice. 'Hie!' he yelled. 'Hie! What are you doing? Who are you?'

He remembered his torch and switched it on. He saw a face he knew, and cried out in surprise. 'Mr. Barling!'

Then someone hit him a hard blow on the head and he remembered nothing more at all. He did not know that he was lifted into the window-seat too. He did not know that the intruder followed after him. He knew nothing.

George, awake in the next room, suddenly heard Sooty's voice crying out. 'Hie!' she heard. 'Hie, what are you doing? Who are you?' And then, as she slipped out of bed, she heard the next cry. 'Mr. Barling!'

George was extremely startled. What was going on next door? She fumbled about for her torch. Anne and Marybelle were still asleep. George could not find her torch. She fell over a chair and banged her head.

When at last she had found her torch she tiptoed, trembling, to the door. She shone her torch and saw that the door next to hers was a little ajar, just as Sooty had left it, when he had crept inside. She listened. There was absolutely no sound at all now. She had heard a small bumping noise after Sooty's last cry, but she didn't know what it was.

She suddenly put her head round the door of her father's room, and shone her torch again. She stared in surprise. The bed was empty. The room was empty. There was no one there at all! She flashed her torch all round.

She opened the cupboard door fearfully. She looked under the bed. She was, in fact, extremely brave.

At last she sank down on the window-seat, frightened and puzzled. Where was her father? Where was Sooty? Whatever had been happening here that night?

Chapter Sixteen

NEXT MORNING

As George sat by the window, on the very seat into which everyone had unaccountably disappeared, though she did not know it, she heard a faint sound from the passage.

Quick as lightning the girl slipped under the bed. Someone was creeping down the long passage! George lay silently on the floor, lifting the valance a little to try and see who it was. What queer things were going on tonight!

Someone came in at the door. Someone stopped there, as if to look and listen. Then the Someone crept over to the window-seat.

George watched and listened, straining her eyes in the darkness. She dimly saw the Someone outlined against the grey square of the window. He was bent over the window-seat.

He showed no light at all. But he made some curious little sounds. First came the sound of his fingers tapping about on the closed lid of the seat. Then came the clink of something metallic, and a very faint squeaking. George could not imagine what the man – if it was a man – was doing.

For about five minutes the Someone worked away at his task in the darkness. Then, as quietly as he had come, he went away. George couldn't help thinking it was Block, though his outline against the dark-grey of the window was too dim to recognize. But he had once given a little cough exactly like Block so often gave. It *must* be Block! But whatever was he doing in her father's room at night, on the window-seat?

George felt as if she was in a bad dream. The queerest
things happened and kept on happening, and they didn't
seem to make sense at all. Where was her father? Had
he left his room and gone wandering over the house?
Where was Sooty, and why had he called out? He
wouldn't have shouted out like that, surely, if her father
had been asleep in the room!

George lay under the bed, shivering, for a little while
longer. Then she rolled out softly and went out of the
door. She crept down the long passage to the end. She
opened the door there and peeped out. The whole house
was in darkness. Little sounds came to George's ears – a
window rattling faintly, the creak of some bit of furniture – but nothing else.

She had only one thought in her mind, and that was to
get to the boys' room and tell them the mysterious things
that had happened. Soon she was across the landing,
and had slipped through the door of Julian's bedroom.
He and Dick were awake, of course, waiting for Sooty
to come with Timmy and George.

But only George arrived. A scared George, with a
very curious story to tell. She wrapped herself in the
eiderdown on Julian's bed, and told what had happened,
in whispers.

They were amazed. Uncle Quentin gone! Sooty disappeared! Someone creeping into the room and fiddling
about on the window-seat! What did it all mean?

'We'll come to Uncle Quentin's room with you, straight
away now,' said Julian, pulling on a dressing-gown, and
hunting about for his slippers. 'I've got a feeling that
things are getting pretty serious.'

They all padded off to the other rooms. They went into
Marybelle's room and woke her and Anne. Both little
girls felt scared. Soon all five children were in the next

room, from which George's father and Sooty had so strangely vanished.

Julian shut the door, drew the curtains and switched on the light. At once they all felt better. It was so horrid to grope about in the dark with torches.

They looked round the silent room. There was nothing there to show them how the others had disappeared. The bed was crumpled and empty. On the floor lay Sooty's torch, where it had fallen.

George repeated again what she had thought she had heard Sooty call out, but it made no sense to anyone. 'Why call out Mr. Barling's name, when there was only your father in the room?' said Julian. 'Surely Mr. Barling wasn't hiding here – that would be nonsense. He had nothing to do with your father, George.'

'I know. But I'm sure it *was* Mr. Barling's name that I heard Sooty call out,' said George. 'Do you think – oh yes, do you think Mr. Barling could possibly have crept through the secret opening in the cupboard, meaning to do some dirty work or other – and have gone back the same way, taking the others with him because they discovered him?'

This seemed a likely explanation, though not a very good one. They all went to the cupboard and opened it. They groped between the clothes for the secret opening. But the little iron handle set there to pull on the stone at the back, was gone! Someone had removed it – and now the secret passage could not be entered, for there was no way of opening it just there!

'Look at that!' said Julian in astonishment. 'Someone's been tampering with that too. No, George, the midnight visitor, whoever he was, didn't go back that way.'

George looked pale. She had been hoping to go and fetch Timmy, by slipping through the secret opening in the cupboard. Now she couldn't. She longed for Timmy with all her heart, and felt that if only the big faithful dog were with her things would seem much brighter.'

'I'm sure Mr. Lenoir is at the bottom of all this!' said Dick. 'And Block too. I bet that *was* Block you saw in here tonight, doing something in the dark, George. I bet he and Mr. Lenoir are hand in glove with each other over something.'

'Well, then — we can't possibly go and tell them what has happened!' said Julian. 'If they are at the bottom of all these queer happenings it would be foolish to go and tell them what we know. And we can't tell your mother, Marybelle, because she would naturally go to your father about it. It's a puzzle to know what to do!'

Anne began to cry. Marybelle, frightened and puzzled, at once began to sob too. George felt tears pricking the backs of her eyelids, but she blinked them away. George never cried!

'I want Sooty,' wept Marybelle, who adored her cheeky, daring brother. 'Where's he gone? I'm sure he's in danger. I do want Sooty.'

'We'll rescue him tomorrow, don't you worry,' said Julian, kindly. 'We can't do anything tonight, though. There's nobody at Smuggler's Top we can possibly get advice or help from, as things are. I vote we go to bed, sleep on it, and make plans in the morning. By that time Sooty and Uncle Quentin may have turned up again. If they haven't, Mr. Lenoir will have to be told by someone, and we'll see how he behaves! If he's surprised and upset, we'll soon know if he has had anything to do with this mystery or not. He'll have to do something — go to the police, or have the house turned upside down to find the missing people. We'll soon see what happens.'

Everyone felt a little comforted after this long speech. Julian sounded cheerful and firm, though he didn't feel at all happy, really. He knew, better than any of the others, that something very strange, and probably dangerous. was going on at Smuggler's Top. He wished the girls were not there.

'Now listen,' he said. 'George, you go and sleep with Anne and Marybelle next door. Lock your door and keep the light on. Dick and I will sleep here, in Sooty's old room, also with the light on, so you'll know we are quite nearby.'

It was comforting to know that the two boys were so near. The three girls went at last into Marybelle's room, tired out. Anne and Marybelle got into bed again, and George lay down on a small but comfortable couch, pulling a thick rug over her. In spite of all the worry and excitement the girls were asleep in a half a minute, quite exhausted.

The boys talked a little, as they lay in Sooty's old bed, where their Uncle Quentin had been asleep some time before. Julian did not think anything more would happen that night. He and Dick fell asleep, but Julian was ready to wake at the slightest noise.

Next morning they were awakened by a most surprised Sarah, who had come in to draw the curtains and bring George's father a pot of early-morning tea. She could not believe her eyes when she saw the two boys in the visitor's bed – and no visitor!

'What's all this?' said Sarah, gaping. 'Where's your uncle? Why are you here?'

'Oh, we'll explain later,' said Julian, who did not want to enter into any details with Sarah, who was a bit of a chatterbox. 'You can leave the tea, Sarah. *We'd* like it!'

'Yes, but where's your uncle? Is he in *your* room?' said the puzzled Sarah. 'What's up?'

'You can go and look in our room if you like and see

if he's there,' said Dick, wanting to get rid of the amazed woman. She disappeared, thinking that the household must be going mad. She left the hot tea behind, though, and the boys at once took it into the girls' room. George unlocked the door for them. They took it in turns to sip the hot tea from the one cup.

Presently Sarah came back, with Harriet and Block. Block's face was as blank as usual.

'There's nobody in your room, Master Julian,' began Sarah. Then Block gave a sudden exclamation and stared at George angrily. He had thought she was locked in her room – and here she was in Marybelle's room, drinking tea!

'How did you get out?' he demanded. 'I'll tell Mr. Lenoir. You're in disgrace.'

'Shut up,' said Julian. 'Don't you dare to speak to my cousin like that. I believe you're mixed up in this curious business. Clear out, Block.'

Whether Block heard or not, he gave no sign of going. Julian got up, his face set.

'Clear out of this room,' he said, narrowing his eyes. 'Do you hear? I have a feeling that the police might be interested in you, Block. Now clear out!'

Harriet and Sarah gave little shrieks. The sudden mystery was too much for them. They gazed at Block and began to back out of the room. Fortunately Block went too, casting an evil look at the determined Julian.

'I shall go to Mr. Lenoir,' said Block, and disappeared.

In a few minutes along came Mr. and Mrs. Lenoir to Marybelle's room. Mrs. Lenoir looked scared out of her life. Mr. Lenoir looked puzzled and upset.

'Now, what's all this?' he began. 'Block has been to me with a most curious tale. Says your father has disappeared, George, and . . .'

'And so has Sooty,' suddenly wailed Marybelle, bursting into tears again. 'Sooty's gone. He's gone too.'

Mrs. Lenoir gave a cry. 'What do you mean? How can he have gone? Marybelle, what do you mean?'

'Marybelle, I think I had better take charge of the telling,' said Julian, who was not going to let the little girl give away all the things they knew. After all, Mr. Lenoir was probably at the bottom of everything, and it would be foolish to tell him what they suspected about him.

'Julian – tell me what has happened. Quickly!' begged Mrs. Lenoir, looking really upset.

'Uncle Quentin disappeared from his bed last night, and Sooty has vanished too,' said Julian, shortly. 'They may turn up, of course.'

'Julian! You are keeping back something,' said Mr. Lenoir, suddenly, watching the boy sharply. 'You will tell us *everything*, please. How dare you keep anything back at a moment like this?'

'Tell him Julian, tell him,' wailed Marybelle, Julian looked obstinate, and glared at Marybelle.

The tip of Mr. Lenoir's nose went white. 'I am going to the police,' he said. 'Perhaps you will talk to *them*, n.y boy. They will knock some sense into you!'

Julian was surprised. 'Why – I shouldn't have thought *you* would want to go to the police!' he blurted out. 'You've got too many secrets to hide!'

Chapter Seventeen

MORE AND MORE PUZZLING

MR. LENOIR stared in the utmost amazement at Julian.
There was a dead silence after this remark. Julian could
have kicked himself for making it, but he couldn't unsay
it now.

Mr. Lenoir opened his mouth to say something at last,
when footsteps came to the door. It was Block.

'Come in, Block!' said Mr. Lenoir. 'There seem to
have been queer happenings here.'

Block did not appear to hear, and remained outside
the door. Mr. Lenoir beckoned him in impatiently.

'No,' said Julian, firmly. 'What we have to say is not
to be said in front of Block, Mr. Lenoir. We don't like
him and we don't trust him.'

'What do you mean?' cried Mr. Lenoir, angrily. 'What
do *you* know about my servants? I've known Block for
years before he came into my service, and he's a most
trustworthy fellow. He can't help being deaf, and that
makes him irritable at times.'

Julian remained obstinate. He caught an angry gleam
in Block's cold eyes, and glared back.

'Well, this is incredible!' said Mr. Lenoir, trying not
to lose his temper. 'I can't think what's come over every-
body – disappearing like this – and now you children
talking to me as if I wasn't master in my own house. I in-
sist that you tell me all you know.'

'I'd rather tell it to the police,' said Julian, his eye on
Block. But Block showed no trace of expression on his
face.

'Go away, Block,' said Mr. Lenoir at last, seeing that there was no hope of getting anything out of Julian while the servant was there. 'You'd better all come down to my study. This is getting more and more mysterious. If the police have got to know, you may as well tell me first. I don't want to look a complete idiot in my own house in front of them.'

Julian couldn't help feeling a bit puzzled. Mr. Lenoir was not behaving as he had thought he might behave. He seemed sincerely puzzled and upset, and he was evidently planning to get the police in himself. Surely he wouldn't do that if he had had a hand in the disappearances? Julian was lost in bewilderment again.

Mrs. Lenoir was now crying quietly, with Marybelle sobbing beside her. Mr. Lenoir put an arm round his wife and kissed Marybelle, suddenly appearing very much nicer than he had ever seemed before. 'Don't worry,' he said, in a gentle voice. 'We'll soon get to the bottom of this, if I have to get the whole of the police force in. I think I know who's at the bottom of it all!'

That surprised Julian even more. He and the others followed Mr. Lenoir down to his study. It was still locked. Mr. Lenoir opened it and pushed aside a great pile of papers that were on his desk.

'Now – what do you know?' he said to Julian quietly. The children noticed that the top of his nose was no longer white. Evidently he had got over his burst of temper.

'Well, sir – I think this is a queer house, with a lot of queer things happening in it,' said Julian, not quite knowing how to begin. 'I'm afraid, sir, you won't like me telling the police all I know.'

'Julian, don't speak in riddles!' said Mr. Lenoir, impatiently. 'You act as if I were a criminal, in fear of the police. I'm not. What goes on in this house?'

'Well – the signalling from the tower, for instance,' said Julian, watching Mr. Lenoir's face.

Mr. Lenoir gaped. It was clear that he was immensely astonished. He stared at Julian, and Mrs. Lenoir cried out suddenly:

'Signalling! What signalling?'

Julian explained. He told how Sooty had discovered the light-flashing first, and then how he and Dick had gone with him to the tower when they had seen the flashing again. He described the line of tiny, pricking lights across the marsh from the seaward side.

Mr. Lenoir listened intently. He asked questions about dates and times. He heard how the boys had followed the signaller to Block's room, where he had disappeared.

'Got out of the window, I suppose,' said Mr. Lenoir. 'Block's got nothing to do with this, you can rest assured of that. He is most faithful and loyal, and has been a great help to me while he has been here. I have an idea that Mr. Barling is at the bottom of all this. He can't signal from his house to the sea because it's not quite high enough up the hill, and is in the wrong position. He must have been using *my* tower to signal from – coming himself to do it too! He knows all the secret ways of this house, better than I do! It would be easy for him to come here whenever he wanted to.'

The children thought at once that probably Mr. Barling *had* been the signaller! They stared at Mr. Lenoir. They were all beginning to think that he really and truly had nothing to do with the queer goings-on after all.

'I don't see why Block shouldn't know all this,' said Mr. Lenoir, getting up. 'It's plain to me that Barling could explain a lot of the queer things that have been happening. I'll see if Block has ever suspected anything.'

Julian pursed his lips together. If Mr. Lenoir was going

to tell everything to Block, who certainly must be in the plot somehow, he wasn't going to tell him anything more!

'I'll see what Block thinks about everything, and then if we can't solve this mystery ourselves, we'll get in the police,' said Mr. Lenoir, going out of the room.

Julian did not want to say anything much in front of Mrs. Lenoir. So he changed the subject completely.

'What about breakfast?' he said. 'I'm feeling hungry!'

So they all went to have breakfast, though Marybelle could eat nothing at all, because she kept thinking of poor Sooty.

'I think,' said Julian, when they were alone at the table, 'I rather think we'll do a little mystery-solving ourselves. I'd like a jolly good look round that room of your father's, George, to begin with. There must be some other way of getting out of there, besides the secret passage we know.'

'What do you think happened there last night?' said Dick.

'Well, I imagine that Sooty went there and hid, to wait until it was safe to try and get into the secret passage as soon as Uncle Quentin was asleep,' said Julian, thoughtfully. 'And while he was hiding, someone came into that room from somewhere, to kidnap Uncle Quentin. Why, I don't know, but that's what I think. Then Sooty yelled out in surprise, and got knocked on the head or something. Then he and Uncle Quentin were kidnapped together, and taken off through some secret way we don't know.'

'Yes,' said George. 'And it was Mr. Barling who kidnapped them! I distinctly heard Sooty yell out "Mr. Barling". He must have switched on his torch and seen him.'

'They are quite probably hidden somewhere in Mr. Barling's house,' said Anne, suddenly.

'Yes!' said Julian. 'Why didn't I think of that? Why, that's just where they would be, of course. I've a jolly good mind to go down and have a look!'

'Oh, let me come too,' begged George.

'No,' said Julian. 'Certainly not. This is rather a dangerous adventure, and Mr. Barling is a bad and dangerous man. You and Marybelle are certainly not to come. I'll take Dick.'

'You are absolutely *mean*!' began George, her eyes flashing. 'Aren't I as good as a boy? I'm going to come.'

'Well, if you're as good as a boy, which I admit you are,' said Julian, 'can't you stay and keep an eye on Anne and Marybelle for us? We don't want them kidnapped too.'

'Oh, don't go, George,' said Anne. 'Stay here with us.'

'I think it's mad to go, anyhow,' said George. 'Mr. Barling wouldn't let you in. And if you did get in you wouldn't be able to find all the secret places in his house. There must be as many, and more, as there are here.'

Julian couldn't help thinking George was right. Still, it was worth trying.

He and Dick set out after breakfast, and went down the hill to Mr. Barling's. But when they got there they found the whole house shut up. Nobody answered their knocking and ringing. The curtains were drawn across the closed windows, and no smoke came from the chimney.

'Mr. Barling's gone away for a holiday,' said the gardener who was working in the next door flower-beds. 'Went this morning, he did. In his car. All his servants have got a holiday too.'

'Oh!' said Julian, blankly. 'Was there anyone with him in the car – a man and a boy, for instance?'

The gardener looked surprised at this question, and shook his head.

'No. He was alone, and drove off himself.'

'Thanks,' said Julian, and walked back with Dick to Smuggler's Top. This was queer. Mr. Barling had shut up the house and gone off without his captives! Then what had he done with them? And why on earth had he kidnapped Uncle Quentin? Julian remembered that Mr. Lenoir had not put forward any reason for that. Did he know one, and hadn't wanted to say what it was? It was all most puzzling.

Meantime George had been doing a little snooping

round on her own. She had slipped into Uncle Quentin's room, and had had a really good look round everywhere to see if by chance there was another secret passage Sooty hadn't known about.

She had tapped the walls. She had turned back the carpet and examined every inch of the floor. She had tried the cupboard again, and wished she could get through into the secret passage there and find Timmy. The study door downstairs was again locked, and she did not dare to tell Mr. Lenoir about Timmy and ask his help.

George was just about to leave the quiet room when she noticed something on the floor near the window. She bent to pick it up. It was a small screw. She looked round. Where had it come from?

At first she couldn't see any screws of the same size at all. Then her eyes slid down to the window-seat. There were screws there, screwing down the top oaken plank to the under ones thàt supported it.

Had the screw come out of the window-seat? Why should it, anyway? The others there were all screwed down tightly. She examined one. Then she gave a low cry.

'One's missing. The one in the middle of this side. Now just let me think.'

She remembered last night. She remembered how someone had crept in, while she had hidden under the bed, and had fiddled about by the window, bending over the polished window-seat. She remembered the little noises – the metallic clinks and the tiny squeaks. It was screws being screwed into the seat!

'Someone screwed down the window-seat last night – and in the darkness, dropped one of the little screws,' thought George, beginning to feel excited. 'Why did he screw it down? To hide something? What's in this window-seat? It sounds hollow enough. It never lifted up. I know that. It was always screwed down, because I remember looking for a cupboard under it, like the one we have at home, and there wasn't one.'

George began to feel certain there was some secret about the window-seat. She rushed off to get a screwdriver. She found one and hurried back.

She shut the door and locked it behind her in case Block should come snooping around. Then she set to work with the screwdriver. What would she find in the window-seat? She could hardly wait to see!

Chapter Eighteen

CURIOUS DISCOVERIES

JUST as she had unscrewed almost the last screw there came a tapping at the door. George jumped and stiffened. She did not answer, afraid that it was Block, or Mr. Lenoir.

Then, to her great relief she heard Julian's voice. 'George! Are you in here?'

The little girl hurried across to the door and unlocked it. The boys came in, looking surprised, followed by Anne and Marybelle. George shut the door and locked it again.

'Mr. Barling's gone away and shut up the house,' said Julian. 'So that's that. What on earth are you doing, George?'

'Unscrewing this window-seat,' said George, and told them about the screw she had found on the floor. They all crowded round her, excited.

'Good for you, George!' said Dick. 'Here, let me finish the unscrewing.'

'No, thanks. This is *my* job!' said George. She took out the last screw. Then she lifted the edge of the window-seat. It came up like a lid.

Everyone peered inside, rather scared. What would they see? To their great surprise and disappointment they saw nothing but an empty cupboard! It was as if the window-seat was a box, with the lid screwed down for people to sit on.

'Well – what a disappointment!' said Dick. He shut down the lid. 'I don't expect you heard anyone screwing down the lid, really, George. It might have been your imagination.'

'Well, it wasn't,' said George, shortly. She opened the lid again. She got right into the box-like window-seat and stamped, and pressed with her feet.

And quite suddenly, there came a small creaking noise, and the bottom of the empty window-seat fell downwards like a trap-door on a hinge!

George gasped and clutched at the side. She kicked about in air for a moment and then scrambled out. Everyone looked down in silence.

They looked down a straight yawning hole, which, however, came to an end only about eight feet down. There it appeared to widen out, and, no doubt, entered a secret passage which ran into one of the underground tunnels with which the whole hill was honeycombed. It might even run to Mr. Barling's house.

'Look at that!' said Dick. 'Who would have thought of that? I bet even old Sooty didn't know about this.'

'Shall we go down?' said George. 'Shall we see where it goes to? We might find old Timmy.'

There came the noise of someone trying the handle of the door. It was locked. Then there was an impatient rapping, and a cross voice called out sharply:

'Why is this door locked? Open it at once! What are you doing in here?'

'It's father!' whispered Marybelle, with wide eyes. 'I'd better unlock the door.'

George shut the lid of the window-seat down at once, very quietly. She did not want Mr. Lenoir to see their latest discovery. When the door was opened Mr. Lenoir saw the children standing about, or sitting on the window-seat.

'I've had a good talk to Block,' he said, 'and, as I

thought, he doesn't know a thing about all the goings-on here. He was most amazed to hear about the signalling from the tower. But he doesn't think it's Mr. Barling. He thinks it may be a plot of some sort against *me*.'

'Oh!' said the children, who felt that *they* would not believe Block so readily as Mr. Lenoir appeared to.

'It's quite upset Block,' said Mr. Lenoir. 'He feels really sick, and I've told him to go and have a rest till we decide what to do next.'

The children felt that Block would not be so easily upset as all that. They all suspected at once that he would not really go to rest, but would probably sneak out on business of his own.

'I've some work to attend to for a little while,' said Mr. Lenoir. 'I've rung up the police, but unluckily the Inspector is out. He will ring me directly he comes back. Now can you keep out of mischief till I've finished my work?'

The children thought that was a silly question. They made no reply. Mr. Lenoir gave one of his sudden smiles and little laughs, and went.

'I'm going to pop along to Block's room and see if he really *is* there,' said Julian, as soon as Mr. Lenoir was out of sight.

He went to the wing where the staff bedrooms were, and stopped softly outside Block's. The door was a little ajar, and Julian could see through the crack. He saw the shape of Block's body in the bed, and the dark patch that was his head. The curtains were drawn across the window to keep out the light, but there was enough to see all this.

Julian sped back to the others. 'Yes, he's in bed all right,' he said. 'Well, he's safe for a bit. Shall we have a shot at getting down the window-seat hole? I'd dearly like to see where it leads to!'

'Oh yes!' said everyone. But it was not an easy job to drop eight feet down without being terribly jolted! Julian went first and was very much jarred. He called up to Dick: 'We'll have to get a bit of rope and tie it to something up there, and let it hang down the hole – it's an awful business to let yourself drop down.'

But just as Dick went to find a rope, Julian called up again. 'Oh, it's all right! I've just seen something. There are niches carved into the sides of the hole – niches you can put foot or hand into. I didn't see them before. You can use them to help you down.'

So down went everyone, one after another, feeling for the niches and finding them. George missed one or two, clawed wildly at the air, and dropped down the last few feet, landing with rather a bump, but she was not hurt.

As they had thought, the hole led to another secret passage in the house, but this one went straight downwards by means of steps, so that very soon they were well below the level of the house. Then they came into the maze of tunnels that honeycombed the hill. They stopped.

'Look here – we can't possibly go any farther,' said Julian. 'We shall get lost. We haven't got Sooty with us now, and Marybelle isn't any good at finding the way. It would be dangerous to wander about.'

'Listen!' said Dick, suddenly, in a low voice. 'There's someone coming!'

They could hear the hollow sound of footsteps coming from a tunnel to the left of them. They all shrank back into the shadows, and Julian switched off his torch.

'It's *two* people!' whispered Anne, as two figures came out of the nearby tunnel. One was very tall and long. The other – yes, surely the other was Block! If it wasn't Block it was someone the exact image of him.

The men were talking in low voices, answering one another. How could it be Block, though, if he could hear as well as that? Anyway, Block was asleep in bed. It was hardly ten minutes since Julian had seen him there. Were there two Blocks, then, thought George, as she had once thought before.

The men disappeared into another tunnel, and the bright light of their lanterns disappeared gradually. The muffled rumble of their voices echoed back.

'Shall we follow them?' said Dick.

'Of course not,' said Julian. 'We might lose them – and lose ourselves too! And supposing they suddenly turned back and found us following them? We should be in a horrid fix.'

'I'm sure the first man was Mr. Barling,' said Anne, suddenly. 'I couldn't see his face because the light of the lantern wasn't on it – but he seemed just like Mr. Barling – awfully tall and long everywhere!'

'But Mr. Barling's gone away,' said Marybelle.

'*Supposed* to have gone away!' said George. 'It looks as if he's come back, if it *was* him. I wonder where those two have gone – to see my father and Sooty, do you think?'

'Quite likely,' said Julian. 'Come on, let's get back. We simply *daren't* wander about by ourselves in these old tunnels. They run for miles, Sooty said, and cross one another, and go up and down and round about – even right down to the marsh. We should never, never find our way out if we got lost.'

They turned to go back. They came to the end of the steps they had been climbing, and found themselves at the bottom of the window-seat hole. It was quite easy to pull themselves up by the niches in the sides of the hole. Soon they were all in the room again, glad to see the sunshine streaming in at the window. They looked out. The marshes were beginning to be wreathed in mist once more, though up here the hill was golden with sunlight.

'I'm going to put the screws back into the window-seat again,' said Julian, picking up the screwdriver, and shutting down the lid. 'Then if Block comes here he won't guess we've found this new secret place. I'm pretty certain that he unscrewed the seat so that Mr. Barling could get into this room, and then screwed it down again so that no one would guess what had happened.'

He quickly put in the screws. Then he looked at his watch.

'Almost dinner-time, and I'm jolly hungry. I wish old Sooty was here – and Uncle Quentin. I do hope they're all right – and Timmy too,' said Julian. 'I wonder if Block is still in bed – or wandering about the tunnels. I'm going to have a peep again.'

He soon came back, puzzled. 'Yes, he's there all right, safe in bed. It's jolly funny.'

Block did not appear at lunch time. Sarah said he had asked not to be disturbed, if he did not appear.

'He does get the most awful sick headaches,' she said. 'Maybe he'll be all right this afternoon.'

She badly wanted to talk about everything, but the children had decided not to tell her anything. She was very nice and they liked her, but somehow they didn't trust anyone at Smuggler's Top. So Sarah got nothing out of them at all, and retired in rather a huff.

Julian went down to speak to Mr. Lenoir after the meal. He felt that even if the Inspector of police was not at the police-station, somebody else must be informed. He was very worried about his uncle and Sooty. He couldn't help wondering if Mr. Lenoir had made up the bit about the Inspector being away, to put off time.

Mr. Lenoir was looking cross when Julian knocked at his study-door. 'Oh, it's you!' he said to Julian. 'I was expecting Block. I've rung and rung for him. The bell rings in his room and I can't imagine why he doesn't come. I want him to come to the police-station with me.'

'Good!' thought Julian. Then he spoke aloud. 'I'll go and hurry him up for you, Mr. Lenoir. I know where his room is.'

Julian ran up the stairs and went to the little landing up which the back-stairs went to the staff bedrooms. He pushed open Block's door.

Block was apparently still asleep in bed! Julian called loudly, then remembered that Block was deaf. So he went over to the bed and put his hand rather roughly on the hump of the shoulder between the clothes.

But it was curiously soft! Julian drew his hand away, and looked down sharply. Then he got a real shock.

There was no Block in the bed! There was a big ball of some sort, painted black to look like a head almost under the sheets – and, when Julian threw back the covers, he saw instead of Block's body, a large lumpy bolster, cleverly moulded to look like a curved body!

'*That's* the trick Block plays when he wants to slip off anywhere, and yet pretend he's still here!' said Julian. 'So it *was* Block we saw in the tunnel this morning – and it *must* have been Block that George saw talking to Mr. Barling yesterday, when she looked through the window. He's not deaf, either. He's a very clever – sly – double-faced – deceitful ROGUE!'

Chapter Nineteen

MR. BARLING TALKS

Meantime, what was happening to Uncle Quentin and Sooty? Many strange things!

Uncle Quentin had been gagged, and drugged so that he could neither struggle nor make any noise, when Mr. Barling had crept so unexpectedly into his room. It was easy to drop him down the hole in the window-seat. He fell with a thud that bruised him considerably.

Then poor Sooty had been dropped down too, and after them had come Mr. Barling, climbing deftly down by the help of the niches in the sides.

Someone else was down there, to help Mr. Barling. Not Block, who had been left to screw down the window-seat so that no one might guess where the victims had been taken, but a hard-faced servant belonging to Mr. Barling.

'Had to bring this boy, too – it's Lenoir's son,' said Mr. Barling. 'Snooping about in the room. Well, it will serve Lenoir right for working against me!'

The two were half-carried, half-dragged down the long flight of steps and taken into the tunnels below. Mr. Barling stopped and took a ball of string from his pocket. He tossed it to his servant.

'Here you are. Tie the end to that nail over there, and let the string unravel as we go. I know the way quite well, but Block doesn't, and he'll be coming along to bring food to our couple of prisoners tomorrow. Don't want him to lose his way! We can tie the string up again just before we get to the place I'm taking them to, so that they won't see it and use it to escape by.'

The servant tied the string to the nail that Mr. Barling pointed out, and then as he went along he let the ball unravel. The string would then serve as a guide to anyone not knowing the way. Otherwise it would be very dangerous to wander about in the underground tunnels. For some of them ran for miles.

After about eight minutes the little company came to a kind of rounded cave, set in the side of a big, but rather low tunnel. Here had been put a bench with some rugs, a box to serve as a table, and jug of water. Nothing else.

Sooty by now was coming round from his blow on the head. The other prisoner, however, still lay unconscious, breathing heavily.

'No good talking to him,' said Mr. Barling. 'He won't be all right till tomorrow. We'll come and talk to him then. I'll bring Block.'

Sooty had been put on the floor. He suddenly sat up, and put his hand to his aching head. He couldn't imagine where he was.

He looked up and saw Mr. Barling, and then suddenly he remembered everything. But how had he got here, in this dark cave?

'Mr. Barling!' he said. 'What's all this? What did you hit me for? Why have you brought me here?'

'Punishment for a small boy who can't keep his nose out of things that don't concern him!' said Mr. Barling, in a horrid sarcastic voice. 'You'll be company for our friend on the bench there. He'll sleep till the morning, I'm afraid. You can tell him all about it, then, and say I'll be back to have a little heart-to-heart talk with him! And see here, Pierre – you do know, don't you, the foolishness of trying to wander about these old passages? I've brought you to a little-known one, and if you want to lose yourself and never be heard of again, well, try wandering about, that's all!'

Sooty looked pale. He did know the danger of wandering about those lost old tunnels. This one he was in he was sure he didn't know at all. He was about to ask a few more questions when Mr. Barling turned quickly on his heel and went off with his servant. They took the lantern with them and left the boy in darkness. He yelled after them.

'Hie, you beasts! Leave me a light!'

But there was no answer. Sooty heard the footfalls going farther and farther away, and then there was silence and darkness.

The boy felt in his pocket for his torch, but it wasn't there. He had dropped it in his bedroom. He groped his way over to the bench, and felt about for George's father. He wished he would wake up. It was so horrid to be there in the darkness. It was cold, too.

Sooty crept under the rugs and cuddled close to the unconscious man. He longed with all his heart for him to wake up.

From somewhere there sounded the drip-drip-drip of water. After a time Sooty couldn't bear it. He knew it was only drops dripping off the roof of the tunnel in a damp place, but he felt he couldn't bear it. Drip-drip-drip. Drip-drip-drip. If only it would stop!

'I'll have to wake George's father up!' thought the boy, desperately. 'I *must* talk to someone!'

He began to shake the sleeping man, wondering what to call him, for he did not know his surname. He couldn't call him 'George's father!' Then he remembered that the others called him Uncle Quentin, and he began yelling the name in the drugged man's ear.

'Uncle Quentin! Uncle Quentin! Wake up! Do wake up! Oh, won't you please wake up!'

Uncle Quentin stirred at last. He opened his eyes in the darkness, and listened to the urgent voice in his ear feeling faintly puzzled.

'Uncle Quentin! Wake up and speak to me. I'm scared!' said the voice. 'UNCLE QUENTIN!'

The man thought vaguely that it must be Julian or Dick. He put his arm round Sooty and dragged him close to him. 'It's all right. Go to sleep,' he said. 'What's the matter, Julian? Or is it Dick? Go to sleep.'

He fell asleep again himself, for he was still half-drugged. But Sooty felt comforted now. He shut his eyes, feeling certain that he couldn't possibly go to sleep. But he did, almost at once! He slept soundly all through the night, and was only awakened by Uncle Quentin moving on the bench.

The puzzled man was amazed to find his bed so unexpectedly hard. He was even more amazed to find some-one in bed with him, for he remembered nothing at all. He stretched out his hand to switch on the reading-lamp which had been beside his bed the night before.

But it wasn't there! Strange! He felt about and touched Sooty's face. Who was this beside him? He began to feel extremely puzzled. He felt ill, too. What *could* have happened?

'Are you awake?' said Sooty's voice. 'Oh, Uncle Quentin, I'm so glad you're awake. I hope you don't mind me calling you that, but I don't know your surname. I only know you are George's father and Julian's uncle.'

'Well – who are you?' said Uncle Quentin, in wonder.

Sooty began to tell him everything. Uncle Quentin listened in the utmost amazement. 'But *why* have we been kidnapped like this?' he said, astonished and angry. 'I never heard of such a thing in my life!'

'I don't know why Mr. Barling has kidnapped *you* – but I know he took me because I happened to see what he was doing,' said Sooty. 'Anyway, he's coming back this morning, with Block, and he said he would have a heart-to-heart talk with you. We'll have to wait here, I'm afraid. We can't possibly find our way to safety in the darkness, through this maze of tunnels.'

So they waited – and in due course Mr. Barling did come, bringing Block with him. Block carried some food, which was very welcome to the prisoners.

'You beast, Block!' said Sooty, at once, as he saw the servant in the light of the lantern. 'How dare you help in this? You wait till my stepfather hears about it! Unless he's in it too!'

'Hold your tongue!' said Block.

Sooty stared at him. 'So you *can* hear!' he said. 'All this time you've been pretending you can't! What a sly fellow you are! What a lot of secrets you must have learnt, pretending to be deaf, and overhearing all kinds of things not meant for you. You're sly, Block, and you're worse things than that!'

'Whip him, Block, if you like,' said Mr. Barling, sitting down on the box. 'I've no time for rude boys myself.'

'I will,' said Block, grimly, and he undid a length of rope from round his waist. I've often wanted to, cheeky little worm!'

Sooty felt alarmed. He leapt off the bench and put up his fists.

'Let me talk to our prisoner first,' said Mr. Barling. 'Then you can give Pierre the hiding he deserves. It will be nice for him to wait for it.'

Uncle Quentin was listening quietly to all this. He looked at Mr. Barling, and spoke sternly.

'You owe me an explanation for your strange behaviour. I demand to be taken to Smuggler's Top. You shall answer to the police for this!'

'Oh no, I shan't,' said Mr. Barling, in a curiously soft voice. 'I have a very generous proposal to make to you. I know why you have come to Smuggler's Top. I know why you and Mr. Lenoir are so interested in each other's experiments.'

'How do you know?' said Uncle Quentin. 'Spying, I suppose!

'Yes — I bet Block's been spying and reading letters!' cried Sooty, indignantly.

Mr. Barling took no notice of the interruption. 'Now, my dear sir,' he said to Uncle Quentin, 'I will tell you very shortly what I propose. I know you have heard that I am a smuggler. I am. I make a lot of money from it. It is easy to run a smuggling trade here, because no one can patrol the marshes, or stop men using the secret path that only

I and a few others know. On favourable nights I send out a signal – or rather Block here does so, for me, using the convenient tower of Smuggler's Top . . .'

'Oh! So it *was* Block!' cried Sooty.

'Then the goods arrive,' said Mr. Barling 'and again at a favourable moment I – er – dispose of them. I cover my tracks very carefully, so that no one can possibly accuse me because they never have any real proof.'

'Why are you telling me all this?' said Uncle Quentin scornfully. 'It's of no interest to me. I'm only interested in a plan for draining the marshes, not in smuggling goods across them!'

'Exactly, my dear fellow!' said Mr. Barling, amiably. 'I know that. I have even seen your plans and read about your experiments and Mr. Lenoir's. But the draining of the marsh means the end of my own business! Once the marsh is drained, once houses are built there, and roads made, once the mists have gone, my business goes too! A harbour may be built out there, at the edge of the marsh – my ships can no longer creep in unseen, bringing valuable cargoes! Not only will my money go, but all the excitement, which is more than life to me, will go too!'

'You're mad!' said Uncle Quentin, in disgust.

Mr. Barling *was* a little mad. He had always felt a great satisfaction in being a successful smuggler in days when smuggling was almost at an end. He loved the thrill of knowing that his little ships were creeping in the mist towards the treacherous marshes. He liked to know that men were making their way over a small and narrow path over the misty marsh to the appointed meeting-place, bringing smuggled goods.

'You should have lived a hundred years or more ago!' said Sooty, also feeling that Mr. Barling was a little mad. 'You don't belong to nowadays.'

Mr. Barling turned on Sooty, his eyes gleaming dangerously in the light of the lantern.

'Another word from you and I'll drop you in the marshes!' he said. Sooty felt a shiver go down his back. He suddenly knew that Mr. Barling really did mean what he said. He was a dangerous man. Uncle Quentin sensed it too. He looked at Mr. Barling warily.

'How do I come into this?' he asked. 'Why have you kidnapped me?'

'I know that Mr. Lenoir is going to buy your plans from you,' said Mr. Barling. 'I know he is going to drain the marsh by using your very excellent ideas. You see, I know all about them! I know, too, that Mr. Lenoir hopes to make a lot of money by selling the land once it is drained. It is all his, that misty marsh — and no use to anyone now, except to me! But that marsh is not going to be drained — I am going to buy your plans, not Mr. Lenoir!'

'Do *you* want to drain the marsh, then?' said Uncle Quentin, in surprise.

Mr. Barling laughed scornfully. 'No! Your plans, and the results of your experiments, will be burnt! They will be mine, but I shall not want to use them. I want the marsh left as it is, secret, covered with mist, and treacherous to all but me and my men. So, my dear sir, you will please name your price to me, instead of to Mr. Lenoir, and sign this document, which I have had prepared, making over all your plans to me!'

He flourished a large piece of paper in front of Uncle Quentin. Sooty watched breathlessly.

Uncle Quentin picked up the paper. He tore it into small pieces. He threw them into Mr. Barling's face and said, scornfully: 'I don't deal with madmen, nor with rogues, Mr. Barling!'

Mr. Barling went very pale. Sooty gave a loud crow of delight. 'Hurrah! Good for *you*, Uncle Quentin!'

Block gave a loud exclamation, and darted to the excited boy. He took him by the shoulder, and raised the rope to thrash him.

'That's right,' said Mr. Barling, in a funny kind of hissing voice. 'Deal with him first, Block, and then with this – this – stubborn – obstinate – fool! We'll soon bring them to their senses. A good thrashing now and again, a few days here in the dark, without any food – ah, that will make them more biddable!'

Sooty yelled at the top of his voice. Uncle Quentin leapt to his feet. The rope came down and Sooty yelled again.

Then there suddenly came the pattering of quick feet, and something flung itself on Block. Block gave a scream of pain and turned. He knocked the lantern over by accident, and the light went out.

There was a sound of fierce growling. Block staggered about trying to keep off the creature that had fastened itself on to him.

'Barling! Help me!' he shouted.

Mr. Barling went to his aid, but was attacked in his turn. Uncle Quentin and Sooty listened in amazement and fear. What creature was this that had suddenly arrived? Would it attack them next? Was it a giant-rat – or some fierce wild animal that haunted these tunnels?

The fierce animal suddenly barked. Sooty gave a squeal of joy.

'TIMMY! It's you, Timmy! Oh, good dog, good dog! Go for him, then, go for him!' Bite him, Timmy, bite hard.'

The two frightened men could do nothing against the angry dog. Soon they were running down the tunnel as fast as they could go, feeling for the string for fear of being lost. Timmy chased them with much enjoyment, and then returned to Sooty and George's father, rather pleased with himself.

He had a tremendous welcome. George's father made a great fuss of him, and Sooty put his arms round the big dog's neck.

'How did you come here? Did you find your way out of the secret passage you've been in? Are you half-starved? Look, here's some food.'

Timmy ate heartily. He had managed to devour a few rats, but otherwise had had no food at all. He had licked the drops that here and there he had found dripping from the roof, so he had not been thirsty. But he had certainly been extremely puzzled and worried. He had never before been so long away from his beloved mistress!

'Uncle Quentin – Timmy could take us safely back to Smuggler's Top, couldn't he?' said Sooty, suddenly. He spoke to Timmy. 'Can you take us home, old boy? Home, to George?'

Timmy listened, with his ears cocked up. He ran down the passage a little way, but soon came back. He did not like the idea of going down there. He felt that enemies were waiting for them all. Mr. Barling and Block were not likely to give in quite so easily!

But Timmy knew other ways about the tunnels that honeycombed the hillside. He knew, for instance, the way down to the marsh! So he set off in the darkness, with Uncle Quentin's hand on his collar, and Sooty following close behind, holding on to Uncle Quentin's coat.

It wasn't easy or pleasant. Uncle Quentin wondered at times if Timmy really did know where he was going. They went down and down, stumbling over uneven places, sometimes knocking their heads against an unexpectedly low piece of roof. It was not a pleasant journey for Uncle Quentin, for he had no shoes on his feet, and was dressed only in pyjamas and rugs.

After a long time they came out on the edge of the marsh itself, at the bottom of the hill! It was a desolate place, and the mists were over it, so that neither Sooty nor Uncle Quentin knew which way to turn!

'Never mind,' said Sooty, 'we can easily leave it to Timmy. He knows the way all right. He'll take us back to the town, and once there we'll know the way home ourselves!'

But suddenly, to their surprise and dismay, Timmy stopped dead, pricked up his ears, whined and would go no farther. He looked thoroughly miserable and unhappy. What could be the matter?

Then, with a bark, the big dog left the two by themselves, and galloped back into the tunnel they had just left. He disappeared completely!

'Timmy!' yelled Sooty. 'Timmy! Come here! Don't leave us! TIMMY!'

But Timmy was gone; why, neither Sooty nor Uncle Quentin knew. They stared at one another.

'Well – I suppose we'd better try to make our way over this marshy bit,' said Uncle Quentin, doubtfully, putting a foot out to see if the ground was hard. It wasn't! He drew back his foot at once.

The mists were so thick that it was really impossible to

see anything. Behind them was the opening to the tunnel. A steep rocky cliff rose up above it. There was no path that way, it was certain. Somehow they had to make their way round the foot of the hill to the main-road that entered the town — but the way lay over marshy ground!

'Let's sit down and wait for a bit to see if Timmy comes back,' said Sooty. So they sat down on a rock at the entrance to the tunnel and waited.

Sooty began to think of the others. He wondered what they had thought when they had discovered that both he and Uncle Quentin were missing. How astonished they must have been!

'I wonder what the others are doing?' he said, aloud. 'I'd love to know!'

The others, as we know, had been doing plenty. They had found the opening in the window-seat where Mr. Barling had taken the captives, and they had gone down it and actually seen Mr. Barling and Block on their way to talk to Uncle Quentin and Sooty!

They had found out, too, that Block hadn't been in his bed — he had left a dummy there instead. Now everyone was talking at once, and Mr. Lenoir was suddenly convinced that Block had been a spy, put in his house by Mr. Barling, and not the good servant he had appeared!

Once Julian felt that he was convinced of this he spoke to him more freely, and told him of the way through the window-seat, and of how they had seen Mr. Barling and Block that very day, in the underground tunnels!

'Good heavens!' said Mr. Lenoir, now looking thoroughly alarmed. 'Barling must be mad! I've always thought he was a bit queer — but he must be absolutely mad to kidnap people like this — and Block must be, too. This is a plot! They've heard what I've been planning with your uncle — and they've made up their minds to stop it because it will interfere with their smuggling. Goodness knows what they'll do now! This is serious!'

'If only we had Timmy!' suddenly said George.

Mr. Lenoir looked astonished.

'Who's Timmy?'

'Well, you might as well know everything now,' said Julian, and he told Mr. Lenoir about Timmy, and how they had hidden him.

'Very foolish of you,' said Mr. Lenoir, shortly, looking displeased. 'If you'd told me I would have had someone in the town look after him. I can't help not liking dogs. I detest them, and never will have them in the house. But I would willingly have arranged for him to be boarded out, if I'd known you'd brought him.'

The children felt sorry and a little ashamed. Mr. Lenoir was a queer, hot-tempered person, but he didn't seem nearly as horrid as they had thought he was.

'I'd like to go and see if I can find Timmy,' said George. 'You'll get the police in now, I suppose, Mr. Lenoir, and perhaps we could go and find Timmy? We know the way into the secret passage from your study.'

'Oh – so *that's* why you were hiding there in the afternoon yesterday,' said Mr. Lenoir. 'I thought you were a very bad boy. Well, go and try and find him if you like, but don't let him come anywhere near me. I really cannot bear dogs in the house.'

He went to telephone the police-station again. Mrs. Lenoir, her eyes red with crying, stood by him. George slipped away to the study, followed by Dick and Julian and Anne. Marybelle stayed beside her mother.

'Come on – let's get into that secret passage and try and find old Timmy,' said George. 'If we all go, and whistle and shout and call, he's sure to hear us!'

They found the way into the passage, by doing the

things they had done before. The panel slid back, and
then another, larger opening came as before. They all
squeezed through it, and found themselves in the very
narrow passage that led from the study up to Sooty's bedroom.

But Timmy was not there! The children were surprised, but George soon thought why.

'Do you remember Sooty telling us there was a way
into this passage from the dining-room, as well as from
the study and Sooty's bedroom? Well, I believe I saw a
door or something there, as we passed where the dining-
room must be, and it's likely Timmy may have pushed
through it, and gone into another passage somewhere.'

They went back, one by one. They came to the dining-
room – or rather, they walked behind the dining-room
wall. There they saw the door that George had noticed
as they passed – a door, small and set quite flat to the wall,
so that it was difficult to see. George pushed it. It opened
easily, and then flapped shut, with a little click. It could
be opened from one side but not from the other.

'That's where Timmy's gone!' said George, and she
pushed the door open again. 'He pushed against the door
and it opened – he went through, and the door fastened
itself so that he couldn't get back. Come on, we must
find him.'

They all went through the small door. It was so low
that they had to bend their heads to go through, even
Anne. They found themselves in a passage rather like the
one they had just left, but not quite so narrow. It suddenly
began to go downwards. Julian called back to the others.

'I believe it goes down to the passages where we used
to take Timmy when we let him down into that pit to go
for a walk! Yes, look – we've come to where the pit itself
is!'

They went on, calling Timmy, and whistling loudly, but no Timmy came. George began to feel worried.

'Hallo! – surely this is where we came out when we climbed down all those steps from the window-seat passage!' said Dick, suddenly. 'Yes, it is. Look, there's the tunnel where we saw Block and Mr. Barling going!'

'Oh – do you think they've done something to Timmy?' said George, in a frightened voice. 'I never thought of that!'

Everyone felt alarmed. It was strange that Block and Mr. Barling could go about unmolested by Timmy if Timmy was somewhere near! Could they have harmed him in any way? They had no idea that Timmy was at that very minute with George's father and Sooty!

'Look at this!' said Julian, suddenly, and he shone his torch on to something to show the others. 'String! String going right down this tunnel. Why?'

'It's the tunnel that Mr. Barling and Block took!' said George. 'I believe it leads to where they've taken my father and Sooty! They're keeping them prisoners down here! I'm going to follow the string and find them! Who's coming with me?'

A JOURNEY THROUGH THE HILL

'I'm coming!' said everyone at once. As if they would let George go alone!

So down the dark tunnel they went, feeling the string and following it. Julian ran it through his fingers, and the others followed behind, holding hands. It would not do for anyone to get lost.

After about ten minutes they came to the rounded cave where Sooty and George's father had been the night before. They were not there now, of course – they were on their way down to the marsh!

'Hallo, look! This is where they must have been!' cried Julian, shining his torch round. 'A bench – with tumbled rugs – and an over-turned lamp. And look here, scraps of paper torn into bits! Something's been happening here!'

Quick-witted George pieced it together in her mind. 'Mr. Barling took them here and left them. Then he came back with some sort of proposal to Father, who refused it! There must have beeen a struggle of some sort and the lamp got broken. Oh – I do hope Father and Sooty got away all right.'

Julian felt gloomy. 'I hope to goodness they haven't gone wandering about these awful tunnels. Even Sooty doesn't know a quarter of them. I wish I knew what's happened.'

Someone's coming!' suddenly said Dick. 'Snap out the light, Ju.'

Julian snapped off the torch he carried. At once they

were all four in darkness. They crouched at the back of the cave, listening.

Yes – footsteps were coming. Rather cautious footsteps. 'Sounds like two or three people,' whispered Dick. They came nearer. Whoever was coming was plainly following the tunnel where the string was.

'Mr. Barling perhaps – and Block,' whispered George. 'Come to have another talk with Father! But he's gone!'

A brilliant light flashed suddenly round the cave – and picked out the huddled children. There was a loud exclamation of astonishment.

'Good heavens! Who's here? What's all this?'

It was Mr. Barling's voice. Julian stood up, blinking in the bright light.

'We came to look for my uncle and Sooty,' he said. 'Where are they?'

'Aren't they here?' said Mr. Barling, seeming surprised. 'And is that horrible brute of a dog gone?'

'Oh – was Timmy here?' cried George, joyfully. 'Where is he?'

There were two other men with Mr. Barling. One was Block. The other was his servant. Mr. Barling put down the lantern he was carrying.

'Do you mean to say you don't know where the others are?' he said, uneasily. 'If they've gone off on their own, they'll never come back.'

Anne gave a little scream. 'It's all your fault, you horrid man!'

'Shut up, Anne!' said Julian. 'Mr. Barling,' he said, turning to the angry smuggler, 'I think you'd better come back with us and explain things. Mr. Lenoir is now talking to the police.'

'Oh, *is* he?' said Mr. Barling. 'Then I think it would be as well for us all to stay down here for a while! Yes, you too! I'll make Mr. Lenoir squirm! I'll hold you all prisoners – and this time you shall be bound so that you don't go wandering off like the others! Got some rope, Block?'

Block stepped forward with the other man. They caught hold of George first, very roughly.

She screamed loudly. 'Timmy! Timmy! Where are you? Timmy, come and help! Oh, TIMMY!'

But no Timmy came. She was soon in a corner with her hands tied behind her. Then they turned to Julian.

'You're mad' Julian said to Mr. Barling, who was standing nearby, holding the lantern. 'You *must* be mad to do things like this.'

'Timmy!' shouted George, trying to free her hands. 'Timmy, Timmy, Timmy!'

Timmy didn't hear. He was too far away. But the dog suddenly felt uneasy. He was with George's father and Sooty at the edge of the marsh, about to lead them round the hill to safety. But he stopped and listened. He could hear nothing of course. But Timmy knew that George was in danger. He knew that his beloved little mistress needed him.

His ears did not tell him, nor did his nose. But his heart told him. George was in danger!

He turned and fled back into the tunnel. He tore up the winding passages at top speed, panting.

And, quite suddenly, just as Julian was angrily submitting to having his hands tied tightly together, a furry thunderbolt arrived! It was Timmy!

He smelt his enemy, Mr. Barling, again! He smelt Block. Grrrrrrrrrr-rrrrrr!

'Here's that awful dog again!' yelled Block, and leapt away from Julian. 'Where's your gun, Barling?'

But Timmy didn't worry about guns. He leapt at Mr.

Barling and got him on the floor. He gave him a nip in the shoulder that made him yell. Then he leapt at Block, and got him down, too. The other man fled.

'Call your dog off; call him off, or he'll kill us!' cried Mr. Barling, struggling up, his shoulder paining him terribly. But nobody said a word. Let Timmy do what he liked!

It wasn't long before all three of the men had gone into the dark tunnel, staggering about without a light, trying to find their way back. But they missed the string, and went wandering away in the darkness, groaning and terrified.

Timmy came running back very pleased with himself. He went to George and, whining with joy, he licked his little mistress from head to foot. And George, who never cried, was most astonished to find the tears pouring down her cheeks. 'But I'm glad, not sad!' she said. 'Oh, somebody undo my hands! I can't pat Timmy!'

Dick undid her hands and Julian's. Then they all had a marvellous time making a fuss of Timmy. And what a fuss he made of them too! He whined and barked, he rolled over and over, he licked them and butted them all with his head. He was wild with delight.

'Oh Timmy – it's lovely to have you again,' said George, happily. 'Now you can lead us to the others. I'm sure you know where Father is, Timmy, and Sooty.'

Timmy did, of course. He set off, his tail wagging, George's hand on his collar, and the others behind in a line, holding hands.

They had the lantern with them and two torches, so they could see the way easily. But they would never have taken the right tunnels if Timmy hadn't been with them. The dog had explored them all thoroughly, and his sense of smell enabled him to go the right way without mistake.

'He's a marvellous dog,' said Anne. 'I think he's the best dog in the world, George.'

'Of course he is,' said George, who had always thought that ever since she had had Timmy as a puppy. 'Darling Tim – wasn't it wonderful when he came racing up and jumped at Block just as he was tying Julian's hands? He must have known we needed him!'

'I suppose he's taking us to wherever your father and Sooty are,' said Dick. 'He seems certain of the way. We're going steadily downhill. I bet we'll be at the marshes soon!'

When they at last came to the bottom of the hill, and emerged from the tunnel in the mists, George gave a yell. 'Look! There's Father – and Sooty too!'

'Uncle Quentin!' shouted Julian, Dick and Anne. 'Sooty! Hallo, here we are!'

Uncle Quentin and Sooty turned in the greatest surprise. They jumped up and went to meet the dog and the excited children.

'How *did* you get here?' said George's father, giving her a hug. 'Did Timmy go back for you? He suddenly deserted us and fled back into the tunnel.'

'What's happened?' asked Sooty, eagerly, knowing that the others would have plenty of news.

'Heaps,' said George, her face glowing. It was so nice all to be together again, Timmy too. She and Julian and Dick began to tell everything in turn, and then her father told his tale, too, interrupted a little by Sooty.

'Well,' said Julian at last, 'I suppose we ought to be getting back, or the police will be sending out bloodhounds to trace us all! Mr. Lenoir will be surprised to see us all turning up together.'

'I wish I wasn't in pyjamas,' said his uncle, drawing the rugs about him. 'I shall feel queer walking the streets like this!'

'Never mind – it's awfully misty now,' said George, and she shivered a little, for the air was damp. 'Timmy – show us the way out of this place. I'm sure you know it.'

Timmy had never been out of the tunnel before, but he seemed to know what to do. He set off round the foot of the hill, the rest following, marvelling at the way Timmy found a dry path to follow. In the mist it was almost impossible to see which place was safe to walk on and which was not. The treacherous marsh was all around them!

'Hurrah! There's the road!' cried Julian, suddenly, as they came in sight of the roadway built over the marsh, running up the hill from the salty stretches of mud. They picked their way to it, their feet soaked with wet mud. Timmy tried to take a flying leap on to it.

But somehow or other he slipped! He fell back into the marsh, tried to find a safe foothold and couldn't. He whined.

'Timmy! Oh look, he's in the mud – and he's sinking!' screamed George, in panic. 'Timmy, Timmy, I'm coming!'

She was about to step down into the marsh to rescue Tim, but her father pulled her back roughly. 'Do you want to sink in, too?' he cried. 'Timmy will get out all right.'

But he wasn't getting out. He was sinking. 'Do something, oh, do something!' shouted George, struggling to get away from her father's hold. 'Oh, save Timmy, quick!'

Chapter Twenty-two

THINGS COME RIGHT AT LAST

BUT what could anyone do? In despair they all gazed at poor Timmy, who was struggling with all his might in the sinking mud. 'He's going down!' wept Anne.

Suddenly there came the sound of rumbling wheels along the road to the hill. It was a lorry carrying a load of goods – coal, coke, planks, logs, sacks of various things. George yelled to it.

'Stop, stop! Help us! Our dog's in the marsh.'

The lorry came to a stop. George's father ran his eye over the things it carried. In a trice he and Julian were dragging out some planks from the load. They threw these into the marsh, and, using them as stepping-stones, the two reached poor sinking Timmy.

The lorry-driver jumped down to help. Into the marsh, crosswise on the other planks, went some more wood, to make a safe path. The first lot were already sinking in the mud.

'Uncle Quentin's got Timmy – he's pulling him up! He's got him!' squealed Anne.

George had sat down suddenly at the edge of the road, looking white. She saw that Timmy would now be rescued, and she felt sick with shock and relief.

It was a difficult business getting Timmy right out, for the mud was strong, and sucked him down as hard as it could. But at last he was out, and he staggered across the sinking planks, trying to wag a very muddy tail.

Muddy as he was George flung her arms round him. 'Oh Timmy – what a fright you gave us all! Oh, how

180

you smell – but I don't care a bit! I thought you were gone, poor, poor Timmy!'

The lorry-driver looked ruefully at his planks in the marsh. They were now out of sight beneath the mud. Uncle Quentin, feeling rather foolish in pyjamas and rugs, spoke to him.

'I've no money on me now, but if you'll call at Smuggler's Top sometime I'll pay you well for your lost planks and your help.'

'Well, I'm delivering some coal to the house next to Smuggler's Top,' said the man, eyeing Uncle Quentin's curious attire. 'Maybe you'd all like a lift? There's plenty of room at the back there.'

It was getting dark now, as well as being foggy, and everyone was tired. Thankfully they climbed up into the lorry, and it roared up the hill into Castaway. Soon they were at Smuggler's Top, and they all clambered down, suddenly feeling rather stiff.

'I'll be calling tomorrow,' said the driver. 'Can't stop now. Good evening to you all!'

The little company rang the bell. Sarah came hurrying to the door. She almost fell over in surprise as she saw everyone standing there in the light of the hall-lamp.

'Lands' sakes!' she said. 'You're all back! My, Mr. and Mrs. Lenoir will be glad – they've got the police hunting everywhere for you! They've gone down secret passages, and they've been to Mr. Barling's, and . . .'

Timmy bounced into the hall, the mud now drying on him, so that he looked most peculiar. Sarah gave a scream. 'What's that? Gracious, it can't be a dog!'

'Come here, Tim!' said George, suddenly remembering that Mr. Lenoir detested dogs. 'Sarah, do you think you'd have poor Timmy in the kitchen with you? I really can't turn him out into the streets – you've no idea how brave he's been.'

'Come along, come along!' said her father, impatient with all this talk. 'Lenoir can put up with Timmy for a few minutes, surely!'

'Oh, *I'll* have him with pleasure!' said Sarah. 'I'll give him a bath. That's what he wants. Mr. and Mrs. Lenoir are in the sitting-room, sir. Oh, sir, shall I get you some clothes?'

The little party went in, and made their way to the sitting-room, while Timmy went docilely to the kitchen with the excited Sarah. Mr. Lenoir heard the talking and flung open the sitting-room door.

Mrs. Lenoir fell on Sooty, tears pouring down her cheeks. Marybelle pawed at him in delight, just as if she was a dog! Mr. Lenoir rubbed his hands, clapped everyone on the back, and said: 'Well, well! Fine to see you all safe and sound. Well, well! What a tale you've got to tell, I'm sure!'

'It's a strange tale, Lenoir,' said George's father. 'Very strange. But I'll have to see to my feet before I tell it. I've walked miles in my bare feet, and they're very painful now!'

So, with bits of tales pouring out from everyone, the household bustled round and got hot water for bathing Uncle Quentin's feet, a dressing-gown for him, food for everyone, and hot drinks. It was really a most exciting time, and now that the thrills were all over, the children rather felt important to be able to relate so much.

Then the police came in, of course, and the Inspector at once asked a lot of questions. Everyone wanted to answer them, but the Inspector said that only George's father, Sooty and George were to tell the tale. They knew most about everything.

Mr. Lenoir was perhaps the most surprised person there. When he heard how Mr. Barling had actually offered to buy the plans for draining the marsh, and how he had frankly admitted to being a smuggler, he sat back in his chair, unable to say a word.

'He's mad, of course!' said the Inspector of Police. 'Doesn't seem to live in this world at all!'

'That's just what I said to him,' said Sooty. 'I told him he ought to have lived a hundred years ago!'

'Well, we've tried to catch him in the smuggling business many and many a time,' said the Inspector, 'but he was too artful. Fancy him planting Block here as a spy, sir – that was a clever bit of work – and Block using your tower as a signalling place! Bit of nerve, that! And Block isn't deaf, after all? That was clever, too – sending him about, pretending he was stone-deaf, so that he could catch many a bit of knowledge not meant for his ears!'

'Do you think we ought to do something about Block and Mr. Barling and the other man?' said Julian, suddenly. 'For all we know they're still wandering about in that maze of tunnels – and two of them are bitten by Timmy, we know.'

'Ah yes – that dog saved your lives, I should think,' said the Inspector. 'A bit of luck, that. Sorry you don't like dogs, Mr. Lenoir, but I'm sure you'll admit it was a lucky thing for you all that he was wandering about!'

'Yes – yes, it was,' said Mr. Lenoir. 'Of course, Block never wanted dogs here, either – he was afraid they might bark at his curious comings and goings, I suppose. By the way – where is this marvellous dog? I don't mind seeing him for a moment – though I do detest dogs, and always shall.'

'I'll get him,' said George. 'I only hope Sarah's done what she said, and bathed him. He was awfully muddy!'

She went out and came back with Timmy. But what a different Timmy! Sarah had given him a good hot bath, and had dried him well. He smelt sweet and fresh, his coat was springy and clean, and he had had a good meal. He was feeling very pleased with himself and everything.

'Timmy – meet a friend,' said George to him, solemnly. Timmy looked at Mr. Lenoir out of his big brown eyes. He trotted straight up to him, and held up his right paw politely to shake hands, as George had taught him.

Mr. Lenoir was rather taken aback. He was not used to good manners in dogs. He couldn't help putting out his hand to Timmy – and the two shook hands in a most friendly manner. Timmy didn't attempt to lick Mr.

Lenoir or jump up at him. He took away his paw, gave a little wuff as if to say 'How-do-you-do?' and then went back to George. He lay down quietly beside her. 'Well – he doesn't seem like a *dog*!' said Mr. Lenoir, in surprise.

'Oh, he *is*,' said George, at once, very earnestly. 'He's a real, proper dog, Mr. Lenoir – only much, much cleverer than most dogs are. Could I keep him, please, while we stay here, and get someone in the town to look after him?'

'Well – seeing he is such a very fine fellow – and seems so sensible – I'll let you have him here,' said Mr. Lenoir, making a great effort to be generous. 'Only – please keep him out of my way. I'm sure a sensible boy like you will see to that.'

Everyone grinned when Mr. Lenoir called George a boy. He never seemed to realize she was a girl. She grinned, too. She wasn't going to tell him she wasn't a boy!

'You'll never see him!' she said, joyfully. 'I'll keep him right out of your way. Thank you very much. It's awfully good of you.'

The Inspector liked Timmy, too. He looked at him and nodded across to George. 'When you want to get rid of him, sell him to me!' he said. 'We could do with a dog like that in our police force! Soon round up the smugglers for us!'

George didn't even bother to reply! As if she would ever sell Timmy, or let him go into the police force!

All the same, the Inspector had to call on Timmy for help before long. When the next day came, and no one had found Mr. Barling and his companions in the maze of tunnels, and they hadn't turned up anywhere, the Inspector asked George if she would let Timmy go down into the tunnels and hunt them out.

'Can't leave them there, lost and starving,' he said.

'Bad as they are we'll have to rescue them! Timmy is the only one who can find them.'

That was true, of course. So Timmy once more went underground into the hill, and hunted for his enemies. He found them after a while, lost in the maze of passages, hungry and thirsty, in pain and frightened.

He took them like sheep to where the police waited for them. And after that Mr. Barling and his friends disappeared from public life for quite a long time!

'The police must be glad to have got them at last,' said Mr. Lenoir. 'They have tried to stop this smuggling for a long time. They even suspected *me* at one time! Barling was a clever fellow, though I still think he was half mad. When Block found out my ideas about draining the marsh, Barling was afraid that once the mists and the marsh were gone, that would be the end of all his excitements – no more smuggling! No more waiting for his little ships to come creeping up in the fog – no more lines of men slipping across the secret ways of the marsh – no more signalling, no more hiding away of smuggled goods. Did you know that the police had found a cave full of them inside the hill?'

It was an exciting adventure to talk about, now that it was all over. The children felt sorry about one thing, though – they were sorry that they had thought Mr. Lenoir so horrid. He was a queer man in many ways, but he could be kind and jolly too.

'Did you know we're leaving Smuggler's Top?' said Sooty. 'Mother was so terribly upset when I disappeared, that Father promised her he'd sell the place and leave Castaway, if I came back safe and sound. Mother's thrilled!'

'So am I,' said Marybelle. 'I don't like Smuggler's Top – it's so queer and secret and lonely!'

'Well, if it will make you all happy to leave it, I'm glad,' said Julian. 'But *I* like it! I think it's a lovely place, set on a hill-top like this, with mists at its foot, and secret ways all about it. I'll be sorry never to come here again, if you leave.'

'So will I,' said Dick, and Anne and George nodded.

'It's an adventurous place!' said George, patting Timmy. 'Isn't it, Timmy? Do *you* like it, Timmy? Have *you* enjoyed your adventure here?'

'Woof!' said Timmy, and thumped his tail on the floor. Of course he had enjoyed himself. He always did, so long as George was anywhere about.

'Well — now perhaps we'll have a nice peaceful time!' said Marybelle. 'I don't want any more adventures.'

'Ah, but *we* do!' said the others. So no doubt they will get them. Adventures always come to the adventurous, there's no doubt about that!